For my mother, Jean Rosemary Reeve,
and her mother, Lilian Whittle, because
they loved the sea.

N
Three Sisters
Whitlake Mouth
Goat Tarn
High Tarn
Mawgan Cove
Dizzard Tor
R. Trollbrook
Stinhall Bay
Trollbrook Mouth
Trollbridge
Compiet's Cove
The Knacker's Knife-rack
Hill Fort
Stack Head
WILDSEA
Stinhall
Crannock Mouth
Stack Bay
Owlsbarrow
Stack
Wheal Tizzy
The Black Hill
Undercliff
Dunes
Stannary
Marazea Bay
Marazea
The Pikelet
Lord Gilpin's Kn
Sundown Watch
St. Chyan's Head
St. Chyan's Common
Long Wood
Merriport Bay
Merriport Hill
Merriport
The Spillikins

1

AT SUNDOWN WATCH

Utterly Dark lay dreaming of the sea. She dreamed she rode the night wind like a gull, gliding out over the cliff's edge, out over the breaking surf in the cove, and far, far out across the western deeps where all the world was water. The huge waves rolled unbroken for thousands of miles, and the moonlight danced along their crests. It was very quiet, except that the waves rustled a little sometimes when one rose too high and its top broke briefly into foam.

'*Utterly,*' the waves were whispering. '*Utterly . . .*'

A rush of white caught her dreaming eye, and she saw that the waves were starting to part around a rock or reef which lay just beneath the surface. The sea grew troubled. It ceased its whispering and began to roar.

'*Utterly! Utterly Dark!*' Fountains of spray smashed upwards; shattered waves were dragged back like sheets of liquid marble from some vast darkness rising slowly, slowly from the depths . . .

Utterly woke with a start. The memory of her dream was already fading, but she could still hear the sea rolling like soft thunder in the cove. She climbed out of bed and felt her way past the washstand and across the room to the window. When she opened the shutters she saw it was still nearly dark outside. A few last stars were lingering above the crown of ancient standing stones on the headland. Yet strangely, although it was so early, she could hear voices. Something had happened to upset the unvarying rhythms of the house, and Utterly sensed that it was something bad.

Perhaps that was what the sea had been trying to tell her . . .

She dressed without bothering to wash, and went padding barefoot along the passage towards the sound of the voices.

Mr and Mrs Skraeveling were both in the kitchen, talking to some men who had come up from Marazea. The men were not used to being in such a grand old house as Sundown Watch. They held their shapeless hats in front of them in rough, red hands, and spoke shyly in low voices. When Utterly came in, they stopped and stood staring at her in a wary, watchful way, like deer poised to run.

Mrs Skraeveling came over and hugged Utterly. It was a consoling sort of hug, but Utterly did not yet know what she was being consoled for. 'You come along with me, little kitten,' said Mrs Skraeveling, leading her out of the kitchen and into the drawing room. There she broke the news which the men had brought from Marazea.

Mr Andrewe Dark, the Watcher on Wildsea, had been drowned.

❖

Utterly was not sure how to feel. Mr Dark was the kind gentleman who had found her washed up on the shore when she was only a baby, and taken her into his home. She could not exactly claim that she had *loved* him, for he had been rather too stiff and sombre and reserved to love. For love she had always turned to Mr and Mrs Skraeveling, who gave it freely, glad of a new child about the place now that all their own had grown and moved away.

But Mr Dark had always been there, one of the three pillars of her life. Each day had begun with him sitting down opposite Utterly in the breakfast room, taking the top off his boiled egg, and saying, 'Good morning, Utterly, I trust you slept well?' Each day had ended with him stomping up the steep stairs of the Tower to make his observations, and then stomping back down an hour later to read in his study. In wintertime, Utterly would look in on him there to say goodnight before she went to bed. In summer, when the Watch was later, he would generally say goodnight before he climbed the Tower. Then Utterly would lie in bed and think of him up there in the Watcher's Loft, and wonder what he was seeing through his telescope . . .

She had never particularly liked those things, or disliked them, or even thought about them at all; they had just been part of the settled, comfortable routine of life at Sundown Watch. Now they would never happen again: the morning egg, Mr Dark's footsteps on the Tower stairs, his gruff goodnight, they all belonged to the past, and Utterly's future seemed suddenly uncertain.

❖

The little church behind the dunes at Marazea was as busy as Christmas for the funeral. Everyone wore their Sunday best, and Mrs Skraeveling had tacked a black taffeta veil to her hat. People had come all the way from Stack and Trollbridge to pay their respects to the Watcher, for it was not every day a Watcher died, and none in living memory had drowned. During Reverend Dearlove's sermon, the women in the pew behind Utterly's discussed the affair in scandalized whispers.

'He was *beachcombing*, they do say, and no good did

ever come of that. The Gorm saw him there, and the sea reached out for him and swallowed him up.'

'Yet he had walked the beaches often enough. You would think he'd be wave-wise, being Watcher and all. And they found the body cast up upon the shore, which proves the Gorm did not want him. If the Gorm decides it wants you, it takes you down into its deeps and there is no body to bury, just a memorial service and the less said the better.'

Then the first woman lowered her voice to an even quieter whisper, so soft that Utterly could barely hear it. 'They say the pockets of his coat were full of *stones* . . .'

Utterly did not see what that had to do with anything. Mr Dark had often filled his pockets with little stones and shells and old corks and all the other curious things he found upon the shore. Sometimes when she was little he had let Utterly go beachcombing with him, and while he picked his way along the tidelines she had amused herself by peeking into the rock pools, where anemones waved their pink arms, and the billowy weeds parted sometimes like curtains of mermaid hair to reveal tiny crabs, or limpets out for a walk, or transparent shrimp, almost too small for even Utterly's sharp eyes to see. It was beautiful in those underwater worlds. Once, Utterly had grown so fascinated that after she had been watching for ages and ages she realized that she had pushed her face down through the pool's surface and was breathing underwater quite contentedly, just like a mermaid.

If only she could have taught Mr Dark that trick, she thought, he would never have been drowned. But Mr Dark had not believed her when she told him about it, and now he lay at the front of the church inside a wooden coffin with brass handles. Utterly had placed a bunch of sea-pinks on the lid. She did not know if Mr Dark had liked sea-pinks, but they grew all over the cliffs around Sundown Watch and she had never heard him say he *disliked* them.

She kept looking at the coffin all through the service, trying to believe that Mr Dark was really in there. It looked too small somehow. But after the last hymn, when Mr Skraeveling and some of the village men lifted it up onto their shoulders to carry it outside, you could see how heavy it was, and that made her realize that poor Mr Dark really was inside it, and that he really was dead.

Outside, a sea wind was blowing clouds across the sky. The graveyard was plunged into shadow each time one passed across the sun. The grass between the gravestones leaned over in the wind, and so did the pink and white daisies that grew in the cracks of the churchyard wall, and the tall, sinister foxgloves which stood sentry upon the top of it. Utterly's long black hair streamed out sideways, for the busy fingers of the wind had undone the ribbon she had tied it with. The white bands of Reverend Dearlove's

6

collar fluttered wildly as he read the funeral service. Mrs Skraeveling held her hat on and dabbed at her eyes with a handkerchief. The other mourners cast sidelong glances at the dunes, as if they half expected the sea to come rushing over them, filling the grave with water before the sexton could fill it with earth.

❖

Everyone Utterly knew was frightened of the sea. That was why there were no harbours on the western shores of Wildsea, no fishing fleet to be seen in Gorm's Bite or Belfriars Bay, and no one throwing in lines or crab pots to catch the crabs and lobsters which thronged there. That was why people lowered their voices when they talked about the sea. That was why none of the cottages in Marazea had windows on the seaward side. That was why you seldom saw anyone strolling on the beach. Most people tried not even to look at the sea, and when they did they just cast nervous glances at it, as though it were a big, fierce animal which might pounce on them at any moment.

And they were right, thought Utterly. The sea *was* a big, fierce animal – but big, fierce animals could be beautiful, couldn't they? She loved the way the great waves moved under the surface of the sea like muscles flexing beneath its chameleon skin. She loved the way it twinkled so merrily on sunny days, and raged so furiously on winter ones. Sometimes she thought she could remember how the sea had gently rocked her up and down in the little boat that had carried her to Wildsea's shores before Mr Dark had found her. She thought the sea remembered that too, because she sometimes sensed it watching her, and sometimes if she woke at night she would lie in bed and listen to the waves whispering *hush, hush, hush* against the shore, and let her own breathing fall into the rhythm of it, until the sea sang her back to sleep.

She wished she could explain those things to the grown-ups. She thought it sad they were so fearful of the sea. If they could not even bring themselves to look at it, then who would take over Mr Dark's duties? Because now that Mr Dark was dead someone would have to take his place. Someone had to be the Watcher on Wildsea.

2

THE WATCHER ON WILDSEA

After the funeral, when Utterly had shaken a great many hands, and made a great many curtseys, and played chase with the Dearlove children behind the church until Mrs Dearlove told them it was not respectful, she decided it was time to broach the subject of the new Watcher with Mr and Mrs Skraeveling. They walked home together up the steep track to Sundown Watch while the western wind blew little glittering showers over them and the stunted trees leaned away from the sea as if appalled.

'What will happen now?' asked Utterly. 'Who will keep the Watch now Mr Dark is dead?'

Mr Skraeveling looked at Mrs Skraeveling, and Mrs Skraeveling looked at Mr Skraeveling. They were a short, sturdy, kindly pair, and they had been married for so long that they had come to resemble each other like matching salt and pepper pots, or one of those couples who wobble out each hour to strike a silver bell on fancy clocks. They had been servants at Sundown Watch all their lives, since before even Mr Dark was born, so Utterly knew the question of who the next Watcher should be must weigh heavily on them. But it seemed they had not found an answer to it yet.

'Maybe Mr Skraeveling could do it?' she suggested.

'Nay, kitten, not I!' said Mr Skraeveling. He pulled off his hat and scratched his round, bald head, troubled at the very idea. ''Twouldn't be proper,' he said. 'An' besides, I haven't enough learning to write the observations in the Log-book every night.'

'Skraeveling can write his own name very neat,' said Mrs Skraeveling loyally. 'But not much more.'

'Anyway,' said Mr Skraeveling, 'Watching is a job for a Dark, and a Dark alone. Always has been, an' always will be. Nay, there is naught else for it: Reverend Dearlove must send word to your uncle William, Mr Dark's younger brother.'

'The one who went away?' asked Utterly.

'That's right, kitten,' said Mrs Skraeveling. 'Master Will went off to school in England the summer before you came to us, when he was no older than you are now. The last we heard of him, he was living in London Town.'

Utterly knew that London was the capital city of England, and since the King of England was also king of all the Autumn Isles, she supposed it was the capital of Wildsea too. There was a coloured print of it on one of the landings at Sundown Watch, and Utterly had often looked at that print and wondered what it must be like to live in a place where there were so many houses and so many people, hundreds and hundreds of people, and all packed in so tightly.

'What does my uncle William do there?' she wondered.

'I am not certain,' said Mrs Skraeveling. 'It is that long since we had any word from him. Master Will never did have much liking for Wildsea, nor Sundown Watch, nor the ancient calling of his family. Still, he will have to come back and take up his duties now, whether he likes it or no. Wildsea cannot be without a Watcher.'

'But it will take weeks for the letter to reach London, and weeks more for Master Will to reach Wildsea,' said Mr Skraeveling. He shook his head. 'I reckon it might be autumn afore there is a Watcher in the Tower again. I've never heard tell of the Watch going un-kept for that long before.'

'Then I will do it myself,' Utterly said.

'You?' said both the Skraevelings, and Mrs Skraeveling added, ''Tis not a fit task for a child, Utterly.'

'I'm not a baby any more,' Utterly reminded her patiently. 'I'm eleven years old, and I can read and write very well. And I am a Dark.'

'That's true,' admitted Mr Skraeveling. He looked at his wife. ''Tis true, Carrie. Poor Mr Andrewe had a lawyer over from Hoyt to fill out the papers all proper like. "*Miss Utterly Dark, the Legal Ward of Mr Andrewe Dark of Sundown Watch on the Island of Wildsea.*" I witnessed it myself,' he added proudly. 'In red ink.'

'But the Watcher ought to be a man,' said Mrs Skraeveling doubtfully.

'I will not be Watcher,' Utterly explained. 'I shall just be keeping the Watch until Uncle William can get here. I bet I shall be very good at it, too.'

Mr Skraeveling seemed ready to agree with her. Mrs Skraeveling looked more doubtful than ever, but she did not say any more about it, for they had reached the top of the track, where a broad ditch and a high grey wall stretched right across the brow of the cliff. Beyond the wall rose the roofs and chimneys of Sundown Watch, with the wooden arms of the old semaphore system on top of the Tower stirring fretfully in the wind.

The ditch and wall had been built to stop sea-witches going out onto St Chyan's Head and lighting their fires among the old stones there, and although there was only one sea-witch left on Wildsea, and she was too old to stir far from her hovel, the gate in the wall was always kept locked. Utterly was about to ask Mr Skraeveling for his key so that she might run ahead and open it, when an extra-strong gust of wind came howling in off the sea and Mrs Skraeveling's hat took flight. 'Botheration!' she cried, as it went soaring away on its black taffeta wings like a bird of ill omen.

Utterly ran after the hat, off the track and onto the rough pasture beyond, but it was flying too high and too fast for her to have much hope of catching it. Then, suddenly, someone who had been sitting as still and silent as a stone in the knee-deep grass rose up right in front of her and plucked the hat from the air as it blew by.

Utterly stopped with a shriek. The stranger held the hat out to her, but Utterly was too nervous to go and take it. The stranger was a woman, very tall and broad, wearing a long cloak which the wind blew out behind her with loud snapping, flapping sounds. Her mane of dark red hair was wind-blown too, and from its thick curls sprouted the wide, five-pointed antlers of a stag.

3

THE TROLL WITCH

'Now what's all this?' demanded Mr Skraeveling, striding over to stand beside Utterly. Mrs Skraeveling followed him, hitching her skirts up as she waded through the wet grass.

The strange woman watched them, still holding Mrs Skraeveling's hat. Her antlers were a sort of hat too, Utterly realized. Now that she had got over the first shock of them she could see the wires to which they were attached shining in the woman's russet hair. It was a peculiar sort of a hat, but then she was a peculiar sort of person altogether. She was one of the troll-people who lived at the north end of Wildsea in the rocky wooded region called the Dizzard. Reverend Dearlove said that it was rude to call them trolls, but Utterly could see why

14

people did, for the woman with the antlers was quite ugly. All the features of her face were too big and too definite, and her thick eyebrows met above her nose. Her eyes were large and deep-set: dark brown eyes with flecks of gold in them.

'I have come to pay my respects to the Watcher,' the woman said. 'I heard the sea had taken him.'

Mrs Skraeveling took back her hat and inspected it suspiciously. Mr Skraeveling said, 'Mr Dark slipped on the rocks down in Blanchmane's Cove a few nights ago and was drowned.'

'I am sorry for it,' said the troll-woman. A flag of old velvet hung from one of her antlers, attached by a thread and fluttering in the wind. 'I saw him often on the beaches,' she said. 'I heard him sometimes, talking to the sea. I never heard it answer him though. I am sorry he is dead.'

'Thank you,' said Mrs Skraeveling.

The woman looked past them at the house which crouched on the clifftop beyond the wall. 'So who will be your Watcher now?' she asked.

'I will,' Utterly told her.

'Now, that's not been decided,' said Mrs Skraeveling.

The troll-woman took one step forward and went down on her haunches to peer more closely into Utterly's face. Around her neck, on cords and strings, hung a collection of curious objects: holed stones, birds' bones, pine cones, the paw of a fox, and many small leather purses and pouches. A smell came from her, not unpleasant, but rich and earthy and very strong. She looked carefully at Utterly. 'You are the child the sea gave to Andrewe Dark,' she said.

'Mr Dark found me on the shore when I was a baby,' Utterly explained. 'I was washed up in a small sort of boat and he took me in so that Mr and Mrs Skraeveling could look after me.'

'Did he now?' said the woman, seeming very interested.

'The child's parents must have been aboard a ship that foundered out in the western deeps,' said Mrs Skraeveling. 'From her looks we think they must have come from China, or Siam, or one of those other places you see pictures of on tea caddies. Perhaps they did not know about the dangers of these seas, poor souls. We thank God they were able to set our little Utterly afloat before their ship went down.'

The antlered woman ignored her and studied Utterly's face again. 'Yes, there is something of the sea about you,' she said, 'but there is something of the land too. That's curious. Most people are either land people or sea people. I am of the land myself, and my name is Aish.'

Aish. It was the sound spent waves made, retreating down a shingle shore, thought Utterly. Or maybe, since Aish was a land person, it was the sound the west wind made as it rushed through the boughs of deep oak woods.

'I'm Utterly Dark,' she said.

Some people laughed when they first heard Utterly's name, but Aish did not seem to think it strange at all, and she went on looking very serious. 'Well, Utterly Dark. My people watched the western sea long before your Tower was built. So you come and find me if you see things stirring there you cannot name. Just call for me in the Dizzard woods, and I will hear.'

Utterly nodded to show she understood. Aish's deep eyes regarded her for a moment longer. Then she snorted like an animal, stood up, bowed her antlers in a dignified way at the Skraevelings, and strode off down the cliff track with her cloak flowing behind her on the wind.

'Well I declare,' said Mrs Skraeveling. 'It is not often we see her kind in this part of the island.'

''Tis a half-day's walk to the Dizzard,' said Mr Skraeveling. ''Twas good of her to come and pay her respects.'

'I have never seen a troll up close before,' said Utterly. 'She had a funny face. She was funny altogether. If she wanted to pay her respects she could just have come to the funeral, couldn't she, instead of waiting here for us? What did she mean about Mr Dark talking to the sea?'

'Perhaps that was just a yarn she was spinning us,' said Mrs Skraeveling. 'I reckon she had crept up here hoping to climb over the wall while we were all in church and go

17

and cast her spells out on the headland among the old stones.'

'Nay,' said Mr Skraeveling. 'Everyone knows the wall is too high to climb without a ladder, which she did not have. Anyway, Dizzard-folk don't hold with sea magic any more than we do.'

'How do we know what they hold with? Wild-wood mad they are, and they live in holes in the ground up in those nasty woods of theirs.'

'But they are gentle enough,' said Mr Skraeveling, who never spoke ill of anyone. 'They are good neighbours, and good farmers, and they make the best cider on the island. They are nothing you need be frightened of, Utterly.'

'I was not frightened,' said Utterly, but she had been, a little, because the troll-woman had seemed so wild, and looked so strangely at her.

Mr Skraeveling gave her his key and she ran to open the heavy gate. In the gardens, wet hydrangea bushes shook themselves like dogs. The showers had pasted leaves to the flagstones of the path leading to the house: the dear old grey house, with patches of orange lichen on its steep slate roofs, and smoke curling out of its tall chimneys. *Atte Sundowne Watch* said the letters on the granite lintel above the big front door, carved there so long ago that it was before people had worked out how to spell properly. And if you looked very closely, as Utterly sometimes did, you could see that there was a little tadpole-shaped comma carved there too, so that the words weren't really saying just the name of the house, they were giving a command: *At Sundown, Watch.*

4

THE TOWER

That evening, as soon as they had eaten dinner, Utterly followed Mr Skraeveling upstairs, taking care to stroke the head of the carved tortoise on the landing newel post as she passed. They went along the corridor past Mr Dark's bedroom and his study, then through the narrow little door which led into the Tower.

The Tower was by far the oldest part of Sundown Watch. It had stood apart from the rest of the house once, until it had been joined to the main building by Mr Dark's grandfather, who had been a great one for making improvements. He had invented the Tower's semaphore system too, which he had used to send messages across the island to Merriport, but you had to climb the hill behind Merriport to see it, and no one bothered any more, so the semaphore arms had not been used for years.

The narrow door opened onto an equally narrow passageway, which led in turn to the narrow stone stair that spiralled up inside the Tower's thick wall. You'd think you were in a lighthouse, Utterly thought as she climbed, but this Tower was for seeing from, not for being seen. At the top of the stairs she scrambled up into the Watcher's Loft and a blur of sea light from the six big windows. The ropes that worked the semaphore arms came down through holes in the ceiling and were wrapped in neat figure-of-eights around brass pegs on the walls. Mr Dark's telescope perched on its tripod as if it was still expecting him to return. The current volume of the Log lay open on the desk beside it.

This was not the first time Utterly had been in the Loft. She had sometimes brought Mr Dark a cup of coffee here on cold nights. 'Thank you, Utterly,' he had always said when she set it down, never taking his eye from the telescope. Utterly had sometimes stood awhile beside his chair, dreading and hoping that tonight might be the night he saw something.

The leather seat of the chair still held the dent his bottom had made, or perhaps his father's bottom, and his grandfather's, and a whole line of earlier bottoms stretching back into the mists of time. Perhaps the Watchers' bottoms shaped themselves to the dent in the chair-seat, rather than the other way about, thought Utterly. But it was far too big a dent for her small behind, and the chair was much too low for her. Mr Skraeveling had brought up a cushion but even so she had to kneel rather than sit on it before she could bring her eye to the eyepiece of the telescope.

'Are you going to be all right up here all on your lonesome?' Mr Skraeveling asked.

'Yes, thank you,' Utterly told him.

'You won't be scared now?'

'Of course not.'

'Nor fall asleep?'

'I have a very important job to do.'

'I'll go down and help Mrs S with the dishes then,' said Mr Skraeveling. 'But if you need anything, kitten, just you shout.'

'I will! Thank you!'

'And you take care on these wicked old stairs when you come down,' he added, from halfway down them.

'I will!' called Utterly. She was keen for him to be gone. It was rather exciting to be up here all on her own, in the highest point on the whole western side of Wildsea.

The Tower commanded a view of the sea from due south to north-north-east. Looking out from its windows was like looking at a map, or a landscape done in miniature. When she looked to her left Utterly could see the coastline reaching away in cliffs and headlands and deep-shadowed inlets, all the way to Gull Point at the southern end of the island. Directly ahead of her, the clifftop on which the house and the Tower stood narrowed to a stony neck which led out onto the promontory of St Chyan's Head and the old stone circle. Turning to her right, she could see the cliff track curving down to where the church, the vicarage, and the low turf-roofed cottages of Marazea dotted the land behind the wide bay called the Gorm's Bite. Beyond that, about seven miles away at the northern end of Wildsea, the rough crags of the Dizzard rose, with twilight already gathering under the trees that clad them, and the blue line of the northern sea just peeking over their rocky summits. Only in the east was the sea hidden to her, blocked by the high hills of Wildsea's interior.

But the east was not the Watcher's concern.

She looked down at the open Log-book, and saw Mr Dark's final entry written there. It was dated the 23rd June, four days ago. *Clear skies, visibility good, the horizon empty.* It was strange to think that, having written those seven words, Mr Dark had gone downstairs, put on his coat, walked out of the house and down onto the shore, and the sea had reached out and taken him. Trying to imagine it, Utterly suddenly recalled what the ladies at the funeral had said. *His pockets were full of stones.*

She leafed back through the book. Mr Dark had once told her that each volume of the Log held ten years' worth of observations. This one was roughly halfway filled, so he must have started it when Utterly was just six and a half. His handwriting was very neat, and not at all difficult to read once you got used to it. Entry after entry, night after night, mostly just a single word or phrase – *Nothing. Nothing. Nothing to be seen. All clear.* Sometimes he had added observations that seemed to have no bearing on his duties – *1st Oct, the geese are flighting, long wavering Vs and Ws of them heading south. 3rd March, the Sea-witch has lit another of her bonfires tonight, down on the Undercliff. The evening star is very bright, close to the crescent of the new moon.*

Utterly turned to the entry for last Christmas to see if Mr Dark had made any note about the new socks she had given him. He had not, which saddened her, for she had spent ages knitting those socks. But a few days later, on the 29th December, she noticed an entry that seemed different from the rest. Even the writing was different, as if Mr Dark's hand had been trembling when he wrote it.

A possible sighting? Rain showers on the horizon but something else behind them – it looked too solid to be cloud.

A few days later, on the first day of the New Year, he had written, *1st January, a light in the west just after sunset, I am very sure of it.*

Utterly turned the pages, scanning the entries. She had a feeling now that she was doing wrong and should stop, as if she were peeking into someone's private diary.

24

But she kept reading anyway, skimming forward through last winter and into the spring just gone.

18th January. Again, in the last of the light, three islands, or is it one with three hills? A light on the shore, perhaps a pale fire burning.

Is it a signal?

Am I expected to answer?

The entries grew more detailed, the pages heavy with ink. Mr Dark had kept writing things and crossing them out, as if what he was seeing – or thought he was seeing – could not easily be explained in words.

16th April. I dreamed she had returned, but the beach was empty.

18th May. We watch and watch and see nothing, or else see things we do not understand. But something out there is watching us, and it sees everything. (This entry had been crossed out, then rewritten and heavily underlined.)

2nd June. The sea speaks to me. She wants back what she has given. Would she accept a substitute–?

The next few entries trailed off in unfinished sentences and violent crossings-out. On the 21st of June, Mr Dark had written, *What does she want?* and underlined it three times. Then on the 22nd and 23rd the observations were perfectly normal again – *Nothing: clear skies, visibility good, all clear, all well . . .*

Utterly wished she had not been quite so eager to let Mr Skraeveling go back downstairs. It was unsettling to think of her guardian, who had always been such a gentlemanly, polite, collected sort of person, writing such odd, feverish things while he was up here alone. It was awfully quiet in the Watcher's Loft, except for the soft sounds of the wind blowing around it, trying the catches on the windows. The rest of the house felt a long way away. Perhaps, she thought, the solitude had disordered Mr Dark's mind. Or perhaps – an even more frightening thought – he really *had* seen the Hidden Lands.

For a moment Utterly felt very afraid, and almost ready to run back downstairs to the cosy warmth of the Skraevelings' little parlour. But she reminded herself firmly that she was almost eleven and a half years old, and that she had a job to do. The sun was sinking low in the west. It was time for the Watcher to make the evening observation. She did not want to give up before she started, and make Mr and Mrs S think she was a baby or a coward.

So she reached for Mr Dark's inkwell, unscrewed the stopper, picked up his pen and dipped it in the ink, then drew a line right across the page of the Log beneath his final entry. Underneath the line, in her very best hand, she wrote: *27th June. Mr Andrewe Dark, the Watcher on Wildsea Island, was found Most Tragickly Drowned 4 days ago. I, Utterly Dark, aged 11 Years & 4 Months, being his Ward, do promise to mantane this Log & Journal until Such Time as the new Watcher arrives.*

5

THE HIDDEN LANDS

It was always at sundown they were seen. In that twilight hour, when the walls between the worlds grew thin, strange things might slip through the cracks. Sometimes then, so the stories went, enchanted islands would appear in the empty ocean to the west of Wildsea. What they were, nobody knew. No ship that tried to sail to them had ever returned. But once, long ago, a sea-witch had lit a fire among the standing stones on St Chyan's Head, and something that dwelled in the Hidden Lands had come raging across the waves to Wildsea: the Gorm – a monster so dreadful that it had been decided a Watcher must be stationed on Wildsea ever after.

It was only a legend. At least, that's what people thought in England, and on more civilized islands like

27

Finnery and Lamontane. But this was Wildsea, on the wind-wracked western edge of the world, where trolls lived in the Dizzard woods and a real live sea-witch still sang her spells down on the Undercliff. On Wildsea it was possible to believe in almost anything.

So Utterly kept her eye to the telescope for an hour each evening, watching the western horizon until it was too dark to see anything at all. She did not see any islands, but nor did she shake off the uneasy feeling that the islands might be there. Again and again she went back to Mr Dark's last entries in the Log, wondering what they could mean. If the Hidden Lands had shown themselves to him, why not to Utterly?

She almost longed for them to appear, but she was not sure what she would do if they did. And what if their appearance heralded the return of the Gorm? The painting of it in the dining room had haunted Utterly's nightmares since she was small, that great scaly roaring monster lumbering out of the surf. Beside the painting hung the antique sword which the first Watcher had used to drive the brute back into the deep. But the sword was longer than Utterly was tall, and looked very heavy. She doubted she could even lift it, let alone use it to save Wildsea if the Gorm came.

She dearly wanted to talk to someone else about what she had read in the Log, but she could not tell the Skraevelings, in case they decided that the job of Watcher was too upsetting for her after all. She thought of going to ask Aish about it, but she was frightened of the troll-woman, and it was a long way to the Dizzard – half a day's walk, Mr Skraeveling had said, which would mean a whole day there-and-back, so she could not go without telling the Skraevelings where she was bound. Then they would want to know why she was going there and it would all come out, so the result would be the same.

The only other people she could have turned to were Reverend Dearlove and his family, who had always been good friends to her. But each time she made up her mind to go down to the vicarage and confide in them she would remember that Mr Dark's pockets had been full of stones . . . When you combined that detail with the peculiar things he had written in the Log, might it not cause Reverend Dearlove to wonder if Mr Dark had gone melancholy-mad and cast himself into the waves deliberately? Then he might have to rouse Mr Dark from his nice neat grave, where the daisies were just beginning to grow, and re-bury him outside the church-yard in the patch reserved for murderers and suicides. Poor Mr Dark! Utterly would not want *that* on her conscience. And what if his ghost came and haunted her afterwards, drifting like a sea-mist up the track to Sundown Watch, all wet from his drowning and a-rattling the pebbles in his pockets? No, that would not do at all.

So she went looking for answers by herself. But all she found were further questions.

❖

Utterly had never spent much time in the upper rooms at Sundown Watch. Her life had been led till now on the ground floor, where her bedroom was, as well as the kitchen, the pantry, the scullery, the dining room and drawing room, and Mr and Mrs Skraevelings' comfortable little quarters. Upstairs had been Mr Dark's domain. Now, Utterly supposed, it must be hers, at least for as long as she was Acting Watcher.

At the far end of the upper floor, next door to the Tower, was Mr Dark's study. It was a deep, narrow room with two long walls of shelves converging on a bay window where an ancient leather armchair waited. The shelves on the left-hand wall, as Utterly stood facing the window, held old volumes of the Log bound in red leather and arranged in ranks like British Grenadiers. Those were not much help to her. They were filled with spiky, spidery notes by Mr Dark and his ancestors. In the oldest volumes the language and the handwriting were so old-fashioned that Utterly could not make them out at all, and in the newer ones, if you took the trouble to decipher them, the entries always turned out to say, 'No sightings', except for a few, marked with red tags, which recorded – what?

Mirages? Mistakes? Madness? Or actual islands, coming and going out there to the west? (Whenever Utterly read *those* entries she always had to take a quick look out of the window, just to make sure the horizon was still empty.)

The shelves on the opposite wall were not much help to her either, but they were far more interesting. There Mr Dark had arranged all the curios which he had found on Wildsea's beaches, protecting them against the dust and moth in glass-fronted boxes or under little crystal domes. There were stones, shells of various sizes, fossils, coral, lumps of amber, long-dead birds, dried fish, and pieces of sea-smoothed wood, which ranged in size from large splinters to small branches. There was a bottle made from a substance that looked like porcelain but was not, and which bore impossibly neat and very tiny writing in an unknown language. There was a box where pieces of brown, green and white glass, washed smooth like pebbles and frosted by long years in the sea, were displayed in matching pairs on a bed of green baize.

There was a case devoted to those leathery black pouches with long trailing points at each corner which Wildsea folk called 'Mermaids' Purses', although Utterly knew for a fact that they were really the egg-sacs of dogfish and other shark-like things. The smallest purse was no bigger than Utterly's thumbnail. The largest was propped up next to the case, because it was far too big to fit inside: an egg-sac the size of a large pillow. When Utterly picked it up it felt smooth and hard and surprisingly light, and when she put her face close to the ragged-edged opening in it she could smell a faint memory of the sea. What sort of monster had hatched out from that?

When the Hidden Lands do Rise, one of Mr Dark's ancestors had written, in a volume of the Log which positively *bristled* with red markers, *strange Tides do Flowe therefrom, and strange Fishes do Swimme therein, and Diverse Beasts are cast up upon the Shores of Wyldesea that do not Belong in this Worlde.*

❖

In the big master bedroom, which had been Mr Dark's, Mr Skraeveling was busy sanding and painting the windows and shutters, making everything ready for Utterly's uncle William when he came home. The dust sheets draped over the dressing table and the washstand gave them the look of rather boxy and unfrightening ghosts.

Utterly sat on the bed and studied the three pictures which hung on the wall. There was a portrait of Mr Dark's father, who looked just like all the other old gentlemen whose portraits hung on the walls of all the other rooms of Sundown Watch: a long gloomy face under a white wig. (Utterly wondered how Mr Dark would be able to pick his father out of the crowd of them when he arrived in Heaven. Perhaps gentlemen did not wear their wigs in Heaven? She would consult Reverend Dearlove on the matter the next time she called at the vicarage.) Beside that portrait hung a likeness of his mother, who had been a very pretty lady with very large, pale grey eyes. The two boys in the third painting had inherited those eyes, along with their mother's (chestnut-coloured) hair. The older of the two was Mr Dark himself - an awkward, gawky lad poised on the brink of becoming a young man. The other boy was still quite little, only five or six. He was William Dark, Utterly's uncle, and she studied him for a long time, wondering what sort of boy he had been, and what sort of man he had become, and what it would be like to meet him.

She imagined herself welcoming him to the Tower and showing him the notes she had made while she had been filling in for him. He was sure to be impressed by how careful her observations were, and how neat her handwriting. He would be just as wise as Mr Dark, but hopefully less gloomy and reserved. Utterly would confide in him, as Watcher to Watcher, and show him the curious notes his brother had made. Then, together, they could puzzle out what it all meant.

6

WILL DARK

'I shall never go back to Wildsea,' said Will Dark, when he read the letter from Reverend Dearlove.

The letter had taken the best part of a month to make its way to London, and been so thoroughly soaked by rain and spray during the journey that it looked as though it had been down with poor Drewe in the deep places of the sea. Unfortunately for Will, its meaning was still clear. *With deepest sorrow . . . regret to inform you . . . his mortal remains recovered from the sea . . . Since this leaves Wildsea with no Watcher, we assume . . . I look forward to welcoming you home . . . yr friend in Christ Jesus, Rev'd Simon Dearlove.*

'I will never go back,' Will told his friends that night, in the Rotunda at the Ranelagh pleasure gardens. The news of Drewe's drowning had shocked him so badly that he could not face spending an evening alone in his rooms, so he had dried his eyes, put on his fashionable new plum-coloured coat, and taken a carriage out to Ranelagh. He could not really afford the carriage, and the food and wine in the Rotunda were damnably expensive, but he told himself that the music, illuminations and cheerful company were just what he needed to lift his spirits. His great friend Frank Constantine was there as always, with a pretty girl on his arm, and there were a half dozen others whom Will knew from the scientific lectures they all attended at the Royal Institution on Albemarle-street. Some were studying medicine, others the Law, and some were as undecided about their future course in life as Will himself, but all considered themselves men of science. They were the sort of friends Will could never have imagined for himself when he was growing up on Wildsea, where such people simply did not exist.

'To my brother Drewe,' he said, raising a glass of the damnably expensive wine. 'God rest his gentle soul, and God bless him for sending me away from Wildsea.'

'Where even is Wildsea?' asked Constantine, when Will told them of his letter. 'We have never heard you so much as speak of your home, Dark.'

Indeed you have not, thought Will. That was one of the things he loved about London. You could spend your days and nights here talking of art, science, politics, the latest plays and the latest scandals, and never have to touch upon where you had come from.

'It is one of the Autumn Isles,' he said. 'They lie so far west of the Scillies that for years they were thought to be no more than sailors' yarns, or a way for bored map-makers to add a little interest to the empty spaces of the Atlantic Ocean. But they are real enough, and Wildsea is the most westerly of them all, a stony place about thirty miles long, and ten across. It is shaped rather like a fish-hook, or a backwards letter J. It has a spine of mountains and a skirt of moor. There's a rocky, wooded region in the north which they call the Dizzard, and actual *trolls* live there, or at least the Wildsea people call them trolls. They live in burrows and are able to work magic.'

'Really?'

'Of course not!' said Will. 'They are just some brutish breed of human, left over from before the Flood, perhaps.' He could see that his listeners were intrigued. He wished he had thought to tell them tales of Wildsea before; he was so seldom able to think of anything witty or interesting to say, and he was enjoying being the centre of attention. The ladies in the party were looking at him quite admiringly. He felt sorry to have disappointed them about the trolls.

'Wildsea is full of such legends,' he assured them. 'Stories are handed down from one generation to the next along with everything else, and everyone believes in them. It's not like a part of England at all. It feels older, and less civilized. Magic seems more real there.'

'Oh, I simply *adore* magic!' said Constantine's companion. 'Are there fairies? I simply *adore* fairies!'

'I would not be surprised,' Will told her. 'There is a certainly a witch – an old madwoman named Thurza Froy who lights fires on the shore and sings spells to the sea. Hundreds of years ago, the legends tell, another of her kind lit a fire on St Chyan's Head, and it woke up something that lived in the uncharted deeps which lie to the west. Those seas are haunted, and all ships that venture on them come to grief. Enchanted islands are said to appear out there sometimes. Those islands are the lair of the Gorm, and when the witch lit her fire she so enraged it that it came swimming to attack Wildsea.'

'What is a Gorm?' asked Carfax, the naturalist.

'Ah, well, the artists who illuminated the old stories have had differing opinions about that,' said Will. 'Some drew it as a giant sea dragon, some as a great vast octopus with too many legs. In the painting on the dining-room wall at Sundown Watch, which used to give me the most horrible nightmares as a lad, it is shown as a sort of lion with a whale's tail.'

'A *sea lion*!' said Constantine, and Will joined in the laughter, happy that his tale was amusing everyone. But beneath his laughter there was the faintest stirring of unease. He really had been very afraid of the Gorm when he was little, and deep down he still was, even though he knew there were no monsters, and that the western sea ate ships simply because that is what seas did.

'But what *was* this Gorm?' the others were asking him. 'What was it *really*?'

Will shrugged. 'I suppose it must have been an earth-quake, or a great wave, and the witch's part in its arrival was mere coincidence. But whatever it was, it caused great death and devastation, and flattened the old town of Marazea completely. Luckily there was a stout yeoman living on the island, by the name of John Dark. He set about the Gorm with a magical sword which he happened to have lying around, as people tended to in Days of Old. The Gorm was bested, and it slunk back grumbling to its own mysterious islands, which promptly vanished again. As a reward, Dark was given leave to build a house on St Chyan's Head, to be held in perpetuity by all his descendants, on the condition that they keep watch.'

'Keep watch for what?'

'For the Gorm's return. For the reappearance of the Hidden Lands. For nothing, probably. Generations of my family have spent each evening gawping at the horizon until their eyes grew dim and their minds filled with peculiar fancies, and never once has there been a firm sighting of any Hidden Lands. We watch because it is the tradition to watch, and traditions are what Wildsea people cling to because they are ignorant fools who are afraid of everything.'

'Oh,' said Constantine after a few moments, realizing that the story was at an end. 'Well, I can certainly see why you left.'

'And why I am never going back,' said Will. His mood had soured. He called for more wine. 'Wildsea will just have to make do without a Watcher. They cannot *force* me to go home.'

❖

But it turned out they could.

Uncertain that his letter would find Will, Reverend Dearlove had sent another to the authorities, and the authorities came knocking on Will's door a fortnight later, in the form of two gentlemen wearing short white wigs and long black coats. They belonged to whichever obscure department of His Majesty's Government looked after the affairs of the Autumn Isles, and they took very seriously the need to maintain a Watcher on Wildsea.

'Why?' asked Will. 'Why do we need to watch any more? The Gorm is only a stubborn old superstition. No educated person believes in the Hidden Lands these days. There is nothing out there. If anyone really thought there were, all Wildsea would be bristling with gun-batteries and Martello forts.'

'You may be right, Mr Dark,' agreed the younger of the two men, who seemed to do the talking for both of them. 'Nevertheless, the common folk may grow restless if they have no Watcher. So as you are the sole surviving heir to Sundown Watch, we should be exceeding obliged if you was to return home and take up your duties there.'

It was not a request. The men watched Will with their calm, unfriendly eyes and waited for him to say 'yes'.

'What if I say no?' he asked.

The man who had spoken made a doubtful face. The man who had been silent leaned forward in his chair and said, 'The schooner *Boldventure* will depart from Falmouth in the second week of August, Mr Dark. She is bound for the Autumn Isles. We have took the liberty of reserving you a cabin.'

7

THE LOOM OF THE LAND

On some evenings the sea was a dark band against the sky. On others the sky was dark and the sea was pale. Sometimes they were both the same, so it was impossible to tell where one ended and the other began. Sometimes steep waves rolled shoreward although there was no wind. Sometimes the wind howled and the waves were small and fierce, and where they broke over the rocks they made Utterly think of white teeth bared in a snarl. Sometimes the sea was as smooth as silk and the setting sun laid a golden road across it. The sea had many faces, and its moods were fickle, and they could change in moments. Sometimes it drew back from the land as if it had lost all interest in it. Sometimes it came rushing loudly in to beat itself against the cliffs and growl. And sometimes as the twilight deepened, sea and sky and land were all one colour, so all that Utterly could observe were a few lighted windows down at Marazea, and a little amber star flickering on the shore beyond, where old Thurza Froy the sea-witch lit her driftwood fires.

❖

July ripened into August, and August wore towards its end, and still Utterly's uncle had not come home. She was starting to think that he would never return. Perhaps he was too busy in London. On the 27th August she drew a little flag beside her entry to mark the completion of her second month as Acting Watcher.

She had stopped expecting the Hidden Lands to show themselves, and when she leafed back through her entries in the Log she could not help but feel they all looked rather samey, for the summer weather had been unusually calm and settled – *22nd July: The sky clear, the sea empty. 23rd July: The sky clear, the sea empty. 24th July: The sky clear, the sea empty* – although on the 5th August she had noted *I saw the old dog-fox catch a rabbit among the standing stones on St Chyan's Head*. She was learning why Mr Dark and the other Watchers had put in little details of that sort before – it added variety, and made the Log feel far more interesting.

But a change was coming. When Utterly went up to the

Watcher's Loft on the evening of the 3rd of September, she saw at once that the western sky looked bruised, and that both sea and air had that ominous stillness that comes before a storm. On the coast north of Marazea a tiny saffron light shone out among the scratchy thickets of the Undercliff. Utterly wondered if Thurza Froy had magicked up the storm, as sea-witches were said to have done in olden days, but she decided it was more likely that the sea-witch had noticed the same changes in the weather that Utterly had, and lit her fire to welcome them.

The sun sank like a hot coal into banks of towering purple cloud on the horizon. As the light faded, Utterly picked up her pen and was all ready to write *Storm clouds in the west, the sea empty*, when she took one last glance at the sea for some reason and saw that it was empty no longer.

Outlined against that swelling mass of cloud was a smaller and still darker mass, humping up from the sea's rim to form three summits. At their lower edge, like a drowned star, a faint pale light was twinkling.

Thunder rumbled, and the clouds flickered inwardly with lightning. Utterly held her breath. She was afraid that her slightest movement might jog the telescope, and that if she lost sight of the mysterious islands she would never be able to find them again. She was shivering. They were only islands, with a lighted window gleaming on the shore of one of them, but they had not been there until a minute ago, and that made them wonderful and alarming, like a vision of Fairyland.

She watched until the approaching storm clouds engulfed them and the light faded and went out. Then she lit her own candle and wrote her observation quickly, before the memory of what she had seen could fade. Before the ink had dried she felt the windows of the Tower flex inward as the first squall struck, and rain came clattering against the glass.

❖

On his voyage from Wildsea to school in England, Will Dark had been terrified. He had never been at sea before, and to be at sea was an awful thing for a boy brought up on legends of the Gorm. He had spent every moment waiting for the deeps to snatch him down.

But twelve years and a knowledge of the natural sciences made the voyage home a far less fearful business. He knew now that the sudden swells which struck the schooner *Boldventure* were not the anger of the Gorm, just cross-currents, or the ripples from some far-off tropic storm. He knew, when the first of the Autumn Isles came into view, that their jagged cliffs had not really been gouged and twisted by great claws, but only by the processes of geology. Indeed, he thought, it was a fascinating proof of the enormous aeons of time which must have passed since the Creation, that so many different strata of rock had come to be layered on top of one another like the slices of bread in one of Mrs Skraeveling's bread-puddings, and then folded and compressed, or turned up-on-end. Studying the cliffs through a telescope from the *Boldventure*'s grubby deck, he almost forgot the lingering echoes of his childish fears.

But there were a great many of the Autumn Isles. Legend told how God's pen-nib had scattered a shower of ink blots while He was drawing up His plans for the world, and rather than start again He had decided to turn each blot into an island. Not all of them featured interesting geology, but each had its squalid little harbour, and the *Boldventure*'s captain seemed intent on calling at every one of them on his way to Wildsea.

Finnery; Lamontane; Gorsedge, Seapitts, Hoyt . . . Will eyed them from the schooner's deck, or ventured ashore on wobbly sea legs to wander their shabby waterfronts, thinking wistfully of London, where the leaves would be settling upon the lake in St James's Park and the ladies putting on their autumn fashions. Each island seemed less civilized than the one before, and ahead of him at journey's end lay only Wildsea, the most backward and dreary of them all.

'Soon be home, sir!' said a sailor, when the *Boldventure* sailed out of Hoyt. Will felt certain that nothing could make him any more miserable, until the storm came roaring up out of the west to prove him wrong.

'Unseasonal weather,' grumbled the captain, looking into Will's cabin at some point during the lurching, roaring, lightless, timeless hours that followed. The captain was drunk as usual. A reek of Finnery whisky wandered into the cabin with him, doing nothing to help Will's seasickness. 'This feels like a midwinter blow, and it's not September yet. Still, we'll get you there, Mr Dark, don't you fret.'

Will didn't believe him, but he was far too miserable to fret. He clung to his bunk, watching a drowned rat bob in the filthy ankle-deep water that sloshed around the cabin floor. He told himself that he should never have left England, but when he tried to remember his life there his numb mind could conjure up only a few faint images: the gleam of sunlight from a dusty mirror in the dining room at his old school in Devonshire, a display of fireworks he had once seen at Vauxhall. The sea had washed all meaning from the memories. He felt absurdly sorry for himself.

At some point, after hours or days, he rolled off his bunk and groped his way up the waterfall of the stairs to the deck. It was dark up there, night-dark as well as storm-dark, he thought, a screeching darkness filled with the savage, unrelenting song of the wind in the rigging. A sudden lurch threw him against the gunwale and he saw white foam a few feet below him. Further off, three vertical white lines glowed faintly in the night like three dim bolts of lightning which did not fade. Will gawped at them while the ship went up and down and up again. Then he understood.

'The Three Sisters!' he yelled.

He remembered walking to them once with Drewe: three tall waterfalls which emptied down the cliffs of the Dizzard, marking the northernmost point on Wildsea. 'Land!' he shouted to the oilskinned, shouting shapes who blundered around on the deck and clung like drenched apes to the rigging. 'Land ho!' (Wasn't that what you were supposed to shout, on ships?) But the wind snatched the words from his mouth, crumpled them up, and flung them overboard. The sailors must have noticed, he thought, trying to tamp down a rising sense of panic. There must be someone on lookout duty at the masthead who would have seen how close they were to shore. The captain must have charts and things which would tell him how sharp the Dizzard's reefs were, and how shockingly far they reached out to sea from between the feet of the Three Sisters.

But Will's first, worst thought had been correct. He was the only one who had seen the loom of the land, and there was nothing he could do about it, and, to be fair, nothing anyone could have done. Not with the wind driving the ship so hard towards the rocks, and the rocks so very sharp, and so very close under the surface.

The jarring crash as she struck flipped Will over the gunwale. He clawed uselessly for a purchase on wet timbers as he fell. Then the sea closed over him and he went down deep, struggling, kicking off his boots as they filled with water and threatened to drag him deeper. His head broke the surface in a trough between two waves. He took a desperate gulp of air which turned out to be mostly salt water. The *Boldventure*'s masts showed black against a burst of spray, surprisingly far away. They looked like letters inked upon the sky. Before Will could read what word they spelled out, the sea took him down again. He swallowed more water, tried to retch, tried to swim, struck out for the surface, but found he had no notion any more of where the surface was.

Strong currents wrestled one another for possession of him. Vauxhall fireworks lit the upturned faces of his friends, who would already be forgetting him. Against the peach-coloured sky of dawn or evening a murmuration of starlings swirled and eddied above the London rooftops. On some long-ago summer morning he was running uphill behind Drewe, towards a hedge bank and a granite stile. He was six or seven, still young enough that each new summer seemed a novelty. He wanted to watch the butterflies, and the hare which he had glimpsed crouching among the wind-blown poppies.

But Drewe ran on ahead, and Will, growing suddenly fearful of the nearby cliff edge and the sea below, ran after him. 'Wait for me!' he shouted, and went after his dead brother down dim galleries of phosphorescent memory into the dark.

8

BEACHCOMBING

By dawn the wind had died away, and the cloud-less sky was stained the same innocent pink as the insides of the shells which the storm had scattered all along the beaches. Broad mirrors of wet sand, revealed by the retreating tide, filled and shone with the reflection of it. All the hunters' paths which zigzagged down the steep flanks of the Dizzard had been turned to little rivers by the rain, and Aish went barefoot down them to the shore.

Aish's people kept away from the sea usually, and Aish knew they were wise to. There could not be much harm in it though, when it was in its present mood, sleepy after its rage the night before. If it had been careless enough to leave any treasures lying on the shoreline, Aish would be able to help herself before it came back to reclaim them.

In Mawgan Cove that morning there were long mounds of weed, the transom of an old boat, and a frayed white thing which might once have been a porpoise. Aish snuffed at the cold air. She had a keen nose. Up on the clifftop she had been able to smell the places a fox had gone questing in the night, and the faint fear-scent of scared rabbits where they had fled into their holes under the brambles. But down here on the beach there was only the stink of weed and the cold, salt smell of the sea.

She was afraid to go too near the water's edge, so she stayed well up the beach and moved along the tideline, kicking at the weed-mounds, scaring up clouds of sand-fleas. White crabs held their delicate pincers aloft like trophies as they sidled out of her way. The freshwater streams which ran across the sand were tea-coloured from the peat washing down off the hills, and so deep Aish had to hitch her skirts up round her thighs to wade across them. She climbed over the rocks at the headland. Offshore, gulls racketed around the summit of the stack called Drowned Man's Pintle. It was so whitewashed with their droppings, it looked like a tall iceberg.

On the sand of the next cove lay an actual drowned man.

He was splayed there like a four-limbed starfish, with the absolute carelessness that only the deeply sleeping and the dead possess. The sea had tried to strip him, as it stripped so many of the people it took, leaving him only his breeches, one stocking and his sodden shirt. His mouth was blue, his face the same dirty white as the little waves which the sea kept pushing up the sand towards him, and his wet hair showed chestnut-colour where it was beginning to dry out.

Aish recognized him, white and blue and sodden though he was. At first she thought he was Andrewe Dark, washing in upon the tide again, but that had happened months ago, at midsummer. That Dark slept now in a good green grave, so this one must be his brother. She remembered seeing the pair of them once, walking together through her woods, when this new-drowned one was just a boy. They had talked and laughed and had no idea that Aish was scrambling through the tree-tops above their heads, delighted with their laughter and their daft clothes and the way the sun lit up their autumn-coloured hair.

She knelt at his side. She sniffed him, but he smelled only of the sea, which had washed his own scent away entirely. He must have been out aboard a boat, she thought, which was a foolish thing to do. You would not catch her venturing out upon the restless, moody ocean with nothing but a boat between her and its cold old hunger. Then she thought how he would have been embarrassed to be seen like this. So although he had been a fool, she felt a sudden deep and pitying tenderness for him anyway, the poor drowndling.

She leaned down her face to his and kissed him. She did not mean to, nor know afterwards why she had done it. Because she was sorry for him. Because she remembered him as a laughing boy in the woods of long ago. Because she felt that someone ought to kiss him, one last time, before the sun grew hot and made him start to stink. But as she touched her warm mouth against his cold one she felt the faintest answering movement there, just enough to make her lift her head and look at him again, and see the quick twitch of his lilac eyelids.

She pressed her fingers to the side of his neck, and there was the faint, frail flutter of a pulse.

So her drowned man was not drowned at all. Aish unpinned her cloak and wrapped him in it, then picked him up – she was strong, and he was only a little small shrimp of a man – and carried him off the beach into the safety of the trees, before the hungry old sea woke up and realized its mistake.

9

THE NEW WATCHER

A young man from the inn at Trollbridge rode up to Sundown Watch while Utterly was washing the breakfast things, and delivered the most exciting news. During the night a ship had come to grief upon Three Sisters Reef, and Utterly's uncle Will had been cast up on the beach, the sole survivor.

'A troll-witch found him there and carried him to the inn,' the young man reported, through a mouthful of the bread and butter Mrs Skraeveling had given him. 'Carried him all the way from Mawgan Cove like he was no more than a sack of taters. He woke up when we got some brandy in him, and was eating eggs and bacon when I left. I am to tell you he will be coming home this very day.'

'Lord be praised!' said Mrs Skraeveling. 'Now come, Utterly, we must air your uncle's room, and make up the bed, and bake a fresh loaf of bread and a pie. Master Will is certain to want feeding up. I am sure there is nothing like being shipwrecked to give a man an appetite.'

There was a frantic morning of activity – spreading sheets, plumping pillows, beating rugs, rolling pastry, sweeping floors, flinging open windows – and then a dull eternal afternoon of waiting. At last, while Utterly was leafing through old books in Mr Dark's study and trying her best not to feel impatient, she heard voices in the hallway, and Mr Skraeveling calling up the stairs, 'Utterly! Master Will is here!'

Utterly threw down her book and ran along the landing, then ran back and scampered up the Tower stairs to fetch the Log, because the new Watcher was sure to want to see it at once. Then she went down again by the back stairs and stopped in at her bedroom so that she could brush her hair and tie it back with the claret-coloured velvet ribbon she had got from Lucy Dearlove for her birthday. She wanted to make a good first impression.

By that time the Skraevelings had led her uncle through into the drawing room, so she went and waited impatiently in the doorway to be introduced. Uncle Will was sitting in Mr Dark's favourite armchair, and Mr and Mrs Skraeveling were standing between him and the door, so Utterly had to peer past them to get a look at him.

He was not as handsome or as tall as she had expected. His chestnut hair was stiff with salt, and the borrowed clothes he wore did not suit him at all, being too large in some directions and too small in others. He sprawled in the armchair in a way that Utterly did not think Mr Dark would have approved of at all – Mr Dark had always told Utterly to sit up straight. But she supposed she must make allowances for Uncle Will, because, after all, he had been shipwrecked.

She took a step forward and made her politest curtsey and said, 'I am very pleased to meet you, sir.'

Her uncle stared at her. Utterly stood smiling at him, holding the current volume of the Watcher's Log against her chest, but Uncle Will did not smile back. He looked at the Log and then at Utterly's face and then at the Skraevelings. 'And who is this?' he asked.

'This is young Utterly, Master Will,' said Mrs Skraeveling.

Uncle Will just stared at Utterly some more. She wondered if she should try another curtsey.

'*Utterly?*' said Uncle Will.

'Your brother's ward,' said Mr Skraeveling helpfully. 'I'm sure Master Drewe must have told you all about her.'

'Certainly not!' said Will indignantly, and then, 'Unless – wait – yes, there was a letter, while I was still at school – page after page of it, something about a lost child that Drewe had taken in. But he did not mention her again – he did not often write – I certainly didn't realize the girl was a *permanent* arrangement . . .'

'Utterly came to us when she was just a baby,' said Mrs Skraeveling. 'Master Drewe made her his ward and said she would bear his name. Skraeveling witnessed the documents himself.'

'In red ink,' agreed Mr Skraeveling proudly.

'And you're quite certain that her name is *Utterly*?' said Will, as if he thought the Skraevelings might have mistaken it somehow.

'That is the name Master Drewe gave her,' said Mrs Skraeveling. 'What name her parents gave her no one knows, for he found her washed up on the shore, the lone survivor of some foundered ship.'

Uncle Will stared some more at Utterly, in a way she thought was rather rude. 'Utterly,' he muttered. 'That was just a joke we had, Drewe and I. We said that if ever we had children we would call them things like "Pitch" and "Inky" and "Utterly". "Utterly Dark", you see . . .' He shook his head. 'It was just a joke. And not even a very funny one.'

Utterly was starting to feel hurt. This was not how she had imagined her first meeting with Uncle Will unfolding, not at all, but she reminded herself again that he was a shipwrecked mariner. 'I am exceeding glad you were not drowned, Uncle William,' she said. 'Was it awfully dreadful being shipwrecked? And is it true that it was

Aish who fetched you ashore? Did she give you any message for me?'

'I did not catch the woman's name,' said Uncle Will. 'She was a . . . one of the Dizzard people. They pointed her out to me at Trollbridge when I woke up. I offered to pay her for carrying me off the beach, but she only smiled at me in a knowing way and shook her head and went back into her woods.' He frowned. 'Why would she have sent a message for you?'

Utterly hugged the Log-book tighter and blushed with pride. 'You see, I have been keeping the Watch, Uncle Will, while we waited for you to come home.'

Rather than thanking her, Uncle Will looked sharply at the Skraevelings. 'That's a bit irregular, isn't it? Isn't the Watcher supposed to be a man?'

'Needs must, sir,' said Mr Skraeveling. 'My old eyes ain't keen enough, I know that much, and Reverend Dearlove is busy with his flock. And young Utterly here is a Dark by name if not by blood, as you might say, and she was keen to help out, so we thought . . .'

'I have made an observation every night,' explained Utterly, 'except for in the storm just past, and on the fourteenth and fifteenth of July when there was a sea fog and nothing to observe at all except the wet on the window-panes.' She went to stand beside her uncle's chair and pressed the Log-book into his hands, opening it to show him the pages she had filled with her neat handwriting.

It must have been a shock for him to find he had an unexpected sort-of niece, she thought, but when he saw how carefully she had been keeping the Watch he was sure to become more friendly.

'Now, kitten, Master Will is too tired to read all those complicated words just yet,' said Mrs Skraeveling.

But Uncle Will was already reading. Utterly watched him, feeling proud of the entries, which she knew almost by heart.

30th August: Mist. Visibility Poor.

31st August: A fine clear evening, there was fishing boats in the far north-east off Whitlake Point, which I could see on account of their lights. The western horizon clear.

1st September: A fine evening, the sea clear all the way to the horizon. I saw a porpus.

The most recent entry, the one which Utterly had made the previous night, was much longer than her others:

3rd September: 8 p.m. I saw three ISLANDS west of Wildsea, or perhaps it may be it was just one low one with three mountains on it. There was a light upon the shore. The ISLANDS stayed visible a full hour, with the light shewing after dark until bad weather hid it.

'What is this?' asked Uncle Will, looking up at her.

'It was the Hidden Lands, sir,' said Utterly, blushing very hotly with excitement. 'I saw the mountains out there very clear, and the light too. Do you think it means the Gorm will come?'

Will shook his head and said firmly, 'No, child, you were mistook. It was low cloud you saw, that's all. A bank of cloud low on the horizon at twilight . . . It is not uncommon, and it can look just like land. I remember being fooled that way myself when I was your age.'

Utterly felt astonished, and then hurt and angry all at once. It was as if he had slapped her. 'But there was a *light*, Uncle,' she insisted. 'It looked like a window shining. I saw it. It was twinkling like a star.'

'Because it *was* a star,' snapped Uncle Will. 'You saw a star shining through a gap in the clouds. That is all.'

'I saw the Hidden Lands!' Utterly insisted, but her voice wobbled, and tears started to come in her eyes, and she knew she did not sound like a sensible, reliable Acting Watcher, but like an angry child.

'You saw clouds,' said Will. He slammed the Logbook shut and stood up. Turning to Mr Skraeveling he said, 'Utterly is a child. While I grant you her eyes may be keen, so too is her imagination. It is easy to let one's fancy spin stars and cloud-banks into islands. That's why my father never let Drewe or I sit the Watch till we were properly trained.'

'Utterly is a bright girl,' mumbled Mr Skraeveling. 'And she has took the job of Watcher very seriously. Your brother would be proud of her.'

'My brother is dead,' said Uncle Will. 'And it was never this girl's job to do. I shall sit the Watch myself tonight.'

60

Utterly started to say something, then stopped herself, and fled from the room before Uncle Will could see her angry tears. She heard Mrs Skraeveling hurrying after her, calling, 'Master Will did not mean it, kitten,' but Utterly knew he had meant every word. In her misery, she even considered the uncomfortable possibility that he might be right, and that she *had* only seen a cloud. But no – she had seen plenty of clouds before: what she had seen last night had been land, as clear and solid as Gull Point or the Dizzard. She darted into her own room, shut the door, locked it, and threw herself face down on her bed to cry.

How could dear Mr Dark, who had always been so genteel and so sensible, have a brother who was so rude and stupid and unkind?

10

DREWE'S POCKETS

Will wandered through the house, and details of it which he had forgotten came back fresh and familiar: a particular cracked flagstone in the hallway, a patch of sunlight on the drawing room wall. The painting of the Gorm still hung above the dinner table, but it had lost its power to frighten him. He had learned something about paintings from his fashionable friends in London. Whatever journeyman artist made this one had known how to do sea, but not much else, and his attempt at a monster was more comical than terrifying.

Beside the picture hung the famous two-handed sword, the Gormblade. Will recalled the words of the old family legend: *There was living then upon Wildsea a bold yeoman named John Dark, to whom the guardian spirit of the isle had gifted an enchanted blade. Taking it in hand, he ventured forth and smote the Gorm upon its foot, so that it was sorely hurt, and went back wailing into the Western Sea* . . . The sword was certainly big, but it looked more like the work of a blacksmith than a spirit, and was clearly hanging out of reach of Mrs Skraeveling's feather duster. Will thought it as cheap and unconvincing as the Gorm.

He climbed the stairs, noticing the brass rods which held the stair carpet in place, the dear old carved tortoise on the newel post on the first-floor landing. He rubbed Tortoise's head for old times' sake, thinking that he was probably the first person to do so since he went away. Then he remembered Utterly. His tortoise would not have been lonely.

He felt sorry now for what he had said to the girl. He realized he should have humoured her about the Hidden Lands. *I was taken unawares,* he assured himself, but he knew that was no excuse.

In Drewe's room, which was now *Will's* room, the smell of the peat fire and the ripply view of the garden and the sea through the thick windowpanes were all just as he remembered. He dressed in the coat and breeches which Mrs Skraeveling had left hanging there for him on a clothes horse in front of the fire. A good brown coat of his brother's, forty years behind the fashion like all the clothes on Wildsea. There were a couple of small stones in the pockets still. Poor old Drewe had always been one for picking up stones.

When Mr Skraeveling looked in to see if all was to his liking, Will said, 'I am afraid I spoke too hastily to the girl,' and waited for the old man to tell him he hadn't, but Mr Skraeveling obviously agreed. 'I was taken unawares,' Will added. 'If I had realized that poor Drewe had adopted a child, if I had been prepared for her . . .'

'She'll come around, Master Will,' said Mr Skraeveling. 'Don't you worry.'

'Where did Drewe find her?' Will asked.

'Why, 'twas down on the shore under Blanchmane's Head. Master Drewe was always a one for beachcombing, as you'll remember, no doubt.'

'Yes, but he used to look for curious shells and old bottles, not children.'

'I can't say what he was looking for, Master Will, only what he found. Our little Utterly washed up with the tide-wrack after a winter storm. It was eleven years since, on the twenty-first of February. I can state that with certainty, for we have taken the twenty-first of February as her birthday ever since, not knowing the real date. Utterly was naught but a babe then. Washed up in a sort of basket she was, so Master Drewe said. He wrapped her in his cloak and carried her home. We reckoned a ship must have foundered in the western deeps, and the poor child's parents managed to set her afloat before they went down with it.'

'Did you ever find out what ship it was? Who her people were?'

'We did not, Master Will. Your brother made enquiries, but I don't think he enquired too hard, for fear she would be taken away from us. We had all grown fond of her, you see. She's a bright little scrap, and those were sad years at the Watch, what with your poor mother and then your father passing away, and yourself gone off to England. The little maid coming to us seemed – well, as I said to Mrs Skraeveling at the time, Master Will, she seemed like exactly what this old place needed to wake it up a bit.'

They stood silently for a moment. Will heard sounds downstairs; Mrs Skraeveling saying something and then the girl's voice laughing. He felt glad that she was happy again, but he still did not understand why Drewe had seen fit to adopt her. Why not just foster her on one of the local farming families? Or, if he had wanted a child, why not take a wife and have children of his own? And as for giving the girl that absurd name . . . *Utterly Dark*. Will suddenly felt a frustration that was very close to grief. If only he could *see* Drewe, *talk* to him. He had no idea what sort of man his brother had become.

'How did Drewe die?' he asked.

'Did they not tell you, Master Will?'

'I had a letter from Reverend Dearlove, but it only said that Drewe had drowned. I don't know how it happened.'

Mr Skraeveling shifted uneasily. 'Master Drewe had been troubled in his mind, sir. Melancholia, you might call it. He had a spell of it twelve years back, after you left

65

us – a black mood came on him then, and he spent all his spare time wandering the shorelines. It passed when he found Utterly, and after that he was himself again. But this year he grew troubled again, and took to his old ways. One night around midsummer, he went down to the cove here after he had finished his Watch, and he did not come back. His body washed ashore on the next tide.'

'He had fallen?'

Mr Skraeveling sighed. Then he said, 'His pockets were full of stones.'

'Drewe's pockets were always full of stones,' said Will. He fetched out a few to demonstrate. The little pale pebbles lay in the palm of his hand like dice. 'He was forever picking things up along the shore. Stones, shells, old potsherds . . . babies . . .'

'That is what the reverend said,' agreed Mr Skraeveling. 'But it was just kindness, so that he did not have to refuse Master Drewe a proper Christian burial in the churchyard. They were proper big cobblestones, Master Will. It was no accident. Your brother filled his pockets with stones to weight himself down, and he walked into the sea.'

11

WATCHING THE WATCHER

Utterly had been expecting everything to return to normal once there was a Watcher on Wildsea again. It would be Uncle Will who would say good morning and good night to her instead of Mr Dark, but otherwise life at Sundown Watch would slip back into its old, familiar rhythm.

But it turned out to be nothing like that. For a start, Uncle Will rose late. Mr Dark had always been in the breakfast room by seven o'clock sharp each day for his boiled egg, but Uncle Will sometimes lay in bed until ten, or even eleven. 'London folk don't rise with the sun like we do, and go to bed soon after it,' said Mrs Skraeveling. 'I heard tell the streets there are lit up with lamps, so no doubt they stay awake till all hours, and sleep in next day to make up for it. And Master Will was in a shipwreck, remember; that must have been very tiring.'

Utterly wondered for how much longer her uncle could go on using his shipwreck as an excuse. When she had the influenza Mrs Skraeveling had made her get up and about again almost as soon as her fever broke, because she said that hard work and exercise was the best way to shake off an illness. Utterly suspected they were the best way to shake off a shipwreck, too. She did not disapprove of Uncle Will's habits though. She was glad he slept late, because it meant she did not have to face him across the breakfast table.

She did have to face him across the dinner table in the evenings, and that was bad enough. Uncle Will was always trying to make conversation with her, as if he hoped to be forgiven for how rude he had been when they first met. 'What have you been doing today, Utterly?' he would ask awkwardly; or, 'It is colder, this evening, is it not?' But Utterly was not ready to forgive him, so she would only answer, 'Nothing very much,' or, 'Tolerable cold, sir,' and the clock would tick, and the knives and forks would scrape on the plates, and Mrs Skraeveling would tell them the latest gossip from Marazea or Stack to break the uncomfortable silence, while the old Gorm goggled down at them from the painting on the chimney breast.

Once Uncle Will said, 'I used to be quite scared of

that old picture when I was a boy. I always tried to sit with my back to it so I did not have to see it, but then I would worry that *it* could still see *me*, and I'd sneak glances over my shoulder to check if it was creeping up on me.' And Utterly, who had done the exact same thing herself when she was smaller, almost found herself saying, 'Me too!' until she remembered just in time that she did not want to have anything in common with Uncle Will, and convinced herself that she had not been so very frightened of the picture after all.

❖

Just like Uncle Will, the September weather seemed to realize that it had been acting the bully with its storms and downpours, and resolved to mend its ways and show Wildsea a kindlier side of its character. The weeks which followed his return were fine, the sky and sea a new-washed blue, the hills green and gold, the berries on the bramble hedges ripening nicely under the autumn sun.

Utterly took advantage of the sunshine to spend as much time as possible out of doors. Sundown Watch did not feel quite like home any more now that Uncle Will was there, and she was afraid that if she hung around the house too much, Mrs Skraeveling would persuade him to take over her schooling, which had been completely forgotten about since Mr Dark was drowned. So each morning, as soon as she had finished her chores, she would walk on the hills, or pick blackberries, or wander down the cliff track and over the dunes to the vicarage.

She had not had much time for the Dearlove children that summer. Lucy and Horatio had hardly seemed suitable company for someone as grown-up and important as the Acting Watcher on Wildsea, and little Emily was still only a baby really. But now she was suddenly Acting Watcher no longer, Utterly was grateful to be welcomed back into their games. The vicarage was not nearly so large as Sundown Watch, but in fine weather the doors and French windows were left open so all the children and their clutter could spill out into the overgrown garden. It was a happy, noisy, untidy little house, where there was always some small emergency going on – 'Emily has swallowed a sixpence!' 'The dog has eaten Father's sermon!' – and the patient, cheerful Dearloves were always setting it right again and never losing their tempers. Utterly wished she could live in such a house, with such a kind mama as Mrs Dearlove, and be part of such a happy family. (She could not imagine what her uncle Will would do if a dog ate something of his. Shoot it, most likely.)

Mrs Dearlove had a cheerful pink face and yellow curls like a porcelain shepherdess, and at present she was busy making preserves, for the fine weather had produced a bumper crop in her fruit cages. Utterly would have liked to try one of the jars of raspberry jam which filled the shelves of the vicarage pantry, but Lucy said, 'They are not for you, Utterly; they are for the Poor. Mama is going to visit all the poor people of the parish and bring them jam. She is even taking some to the sea-witch, and I am going to go with her, because I have never met a real, live witch before. I am hoping she will turn Horatio into a crab.'

'I hope she does,' said Horatio. 'I shall make a very splendid crab, and have a fine time nipping your fat toes with my pincers.'

'Children, children!' said Mrs Dearlove vaguely, before they began to squabble. 'Utterly, I daresay your uncle has many fascinating stories of his time in England? Perhaps we should ask him to luncheon one day so that he can tell them to Lucy and Horatio. I cannot get either of them to take the slightest interest in history or geography.'

But Utterly did not want Uncle Will following her to the vicarage, which was her favourite refuge from him, and taking her friends for himself the same way he had taken her job, so she thought fast and said, 'I think Uncle William is *much* too busy, Mrs Dearlove. He has all the Logs from all the years he was away to read through, and at least a dozen other things.'

❖

But the strange thing was, Uncle William did not seem very interested in the Logs. He did not seem very interested in keeping the Watch at all. Each evening after dinner he would push back his chair, say, 'Time to do my duty,' and climb the Tower to the Watcher's Loft, but often, before the last light had completely faded from the sea, he would be back downstairs, sitting by the fire and reading a novel or a book of poems. One night at the beginning of October, when patchy mist had veiled the sea all day, he had come down from the Tower after less than a quarter-hour and announced, 'Nothing doing tonight.'

Utterly was shocked, and she could tell that Mr and Mrs Skraeveling were shocked too. Surely Uncle Will must know that it was the Watcher's solemn duty to keep his Watch till darkness fell, whether he could see anything or not, just in case some momentary change in the weather should reveal a glimpse of the Hidden Lands?

That made Utterly wonder if this new Watcher was even keeping a proper Log, or bothering to polish the telescope and do the other small chores which he was supposed to. So the next morning, while Uncle Will was still in bed, she climbed the Tower herself to check.

It was the first time she had set foot in the Watcher's Loft since her uncle's return. She was glad to see that it was much as she had left it. The telescope on its tripod looked shiny enough, and Uncle Will had made a note in the Log every night, though Utterly considered that his hand was not as neat as hers, and his entries tended to be terse. *Nothing*, he had written, on most of the nights since his arrival, and sometimes he had not even bothered to write that, just put *ditto* or *see above* beneath the previous night's *Nothing*.

Lying beside the open Log was a page of foolscap covered in rather neater writing, and Utterly had read the first paragraph or two before she realized that it was a personal letter to someone in London. Uncle Will wrote a lot of letters to people in England, which he took down to the inn at Marazea to be carried over the hills to Merriport and put aboard a boat. Utterly did not see much point – Uncle Will was such a dull and dislikeable young man that she was sure everyone he knew in England had breathed a sigh of relief when he left, and would have forgotten who he even was by now. Still, she was curious to know what he wrote to them *about*. She knew it was wrong to read other people's correspondence, but she also knew it was wrong for a Watcher to spend his Watch writing letters when he was supposed to keep his eyes and his mind on the sea, so she did not feel too guilty about reading what he had written.

My dear Constantine,

Everything here on Wildsea continues to be dreary. I have no intelligent company at all, and nothing ever happens. How I miss the hectic pace of life in London, where we might visit a new coffee house one day and go back a week later to find that it has changed hands, or become a barber's, or a bookseller, or been knocked down entirely to make way for a row of brand-new houses! Here almost everything is just as I left it twelve years ago.

That made Utterly pause. It had not occurred to her that Uncle Will might be lonely or unhappy. For a moment she felt dangerously inclined to feel sorry for him. But the line about 'no intelligent company' reminded her that he was a villain after all. ('No intelligent company', indeed! What about the Skraevelings? What about Reverend and Mrs Dearlove? What about *Utterly herself*?) So she read on.

At least the weather smiles on me. Each afternoon I walk out to Marazea, or Stinhall, or to the Stag-Headed Oak at Owlsbarrow. I watch cloud-shadows sweep across the hills, and pretend that the sea is a hundred miles away. But ever the shadows lengthen, and I must start back to sit Watch as the evening draws on. And to sit Watch for what? Why, for nothing. For an imaginary monster, and some fairy islands which every man of reason in this modern age knows full well do not exist and never did. I imagine Government believes the Wildsea folk would raise a rumpus was Sundown Watch to be shut up and your obedient servant permitted to return to livelier pursuits in England – but surely they could find some other poor fellow to be Watcher?

The letter ended there in a flurry of scribbled-out words – perhaps Uncle Will had planned to finish it the next evening, or perhaps he had abandoned this draft and made a clean copy – but it did not signify, because Utterly had already learned the worst. The new Watcher on Wildsea did not believe in the Hidden Lands or in the Gorm. And whatever was the use of a Watcher who did not believe in the very things he was supposed to be Watching for?

Utterly thought of the old stories. She thought of the great Gorm stirring from its slumbers upon the shores of the Hidden Lands. What awful luck it was, that in this time of growing danger, the Watcher on Wildsea should be her stupid uncle. He probably wouldn't believe in the Gorm even if it reared up out of the deeps and waved a cheery tentacle at him.

She sat down in the Watcher's chair, in the hollow shaped by the bottoms of all Uncle Will's forefathers. She knew with a fearful but faintly thrilling certainty what she must do. Wildsea's safety depended on her. If Uncle Will would not do his duty properly, then she would just have to go on doing it for him.

From now on, she must keep her own Watch.

12

THE STRONGBOX

The autumn days were long and warm, but the evenings were chill. When Mr Skraeveling lit the fires each afternoon the smell brought Will's childhood memories fluttering out of the corners of the rooms like the confused butterflies which appeared occasionally at dinnertime, lured from their snug perches in the curtains by the warmth.

It had not been a happy childhood. He had been so scared of the sea, so scared of the Gorm, and so scared of his father, a stern man who it was said had never smiled again after Will's mother died (although, to be fair, Will did not believe he had ever smiled much when she was living, either).

What in their childhoods had persuaded his brother

that Sundown Watch would be a suitable place to raise a child? Will kept trying to understand it, but he could not. If Utterly had been a boy it might have made sense, for with Will gone the Darks had need of an heir, but a girl could not grow up to be the next Watcher. Was it possible his brother had got some Wildsea woman with child, and made up the tale about the basket to conceal it?

He studied Utterly carefully across the table each evening at dinner. She was neither a pretty child nor exactly a plain one, but sometimes, in her watchful dark eyes or the tilt of her head, he thought he glimpsed a faint resemblance to Drewe.

❖

Will slept badly, those first few weeks. He turned in as late as possible each night, hoping to tire himself out, but no sooner did he close his eyes than he would find himself back aboard the *Boldventure* as she struck Three Sisters Reef, and he would wake shivering with terror.

What is the sea for? he wondered sometimes, lying there listening to it rasp and sigh against the cliffs. *We cannot live in it. We cannot drink it. We cannot mine it or farm it. Travelling upon it or fishing in it are both deadly dangerous occupations. What sort of God would give over seven-tenths of His creation to such a restless and unreasonable element?*

One night, despairing of ever getting back to sleep,

he lit a candle and went along the passage to the study. If Utterly *was* Drewe's secret child then perhaps there would be some clue in the Log as to who her mother might have been. He lifted one of the old volumes down from its shelf, blew the dust off it, and began turning back through the heavy pages to the date when Mr Skraeveling had said the girl washed ashore: the 21st of February eleven years before.

There, at the top of a right-hand page, Drewe had written, *A low mist made observation impossible, but although it showed me no Hidden Lands, the sea did present me with something of interest today. Walking on the shore at Blanchmane's Head, I discovered a small wicker boat or coracle which had been carried there on last night's tide. Inside it, wrapped in oilskins, lay a female infant. The child appears healthy – I hear her bawling lustily for her supper as I write. Mrs Skraeveling will care for her & I shall make enquiries lest she was washed overboard from some passing ship. But that seems unlikely – so few ships pass west of Wildsea, and those that do are seldom heard of again.*

And that was all. Will leafed back through the entries from the previous year, but they were all routine, except for the 17th of March, when Drewe had added a note which read, *My brother, William Dark, left us today. He will travel by packet to Falmouth, and thence by mail-coach to school in Devonshire. He will be missed.*

Poor Drewe, Will thought. I was so eager to get away

from this place and see the world, I never stopped to think that he might miss me.

He put the Log back in its place and turned to study the collection of curios and relics Drewe had gathered from the tidelines. If a baby had washed ashore in a coracle, he thought, his brother would have been more likely to keep the coracle and throw away the baby. But there was no coracle in the collection, nor anything that resembled one.

Standing on a chair to peer to the back of the topmost shelf, Will saw that a box had been pushed far back into the shadows there. An old oak strongbox: iron-bound, and studded with square-headed nails. The box was heavy, hard to drag out into the light, and, as it turned out when Will finally did so, locked.

The next morning at breakfast Will quizzed Mr Skraeveling about the box, but Skraeveling knew nothing of it, nor where any key to it could be found. 'I could break it open for you, Master Will,' he offered.

'It doesn't matter,' said Will. He was suddenly weary of the whole puzzle. He could hear Utterly singing a song about horses while she helped Mrs Skraeveling in the kitchen. The girl was happy here. What did it matter whose daughter she was? Whatever was locked up in that box was something Drewe had wanted to stay secret. I have pried too much into Drewe's private affairs, he thought. Let this be an end to it. I am glad there is no key.

13

THE SECRET WATCH

The view from Utterly's bedroom window was nothing like so extensive as her view from the Tower had been, but the portion of the horizon which she could see was the same portion where she had seen the Hidden Lands, and she felt sure that if she was patient she would see them there again. Then she would go and find Uncle William and point out the islands to him – the islands with their three peaks, just as she had written in the Log – and he would have to say, 'Yes, Utterly, you are right: you are *utterly* right, and I am a fool, and a rude one to boot.' That was how it always worked out in stories – the wise girl was rewarded, and the foolish grown-up who had doubted her cast down.

It was a pleasant prospect, but there was one problem.

For days and days after Utterly started keeping her secret Watch, the sea remained empty of everything but the long path which was laid on it each evening by the westering sun.

Utterly felt annoyed, but also uneasy. There was *something* out there, she was certain. She could feel it. She imagined the Hidden Lands appearing when her back was turned, and then vanishing again the moment she looked round, just to tease her. Except she knew the Hidden Lands would never tease. They were far too old and strange and serious for that.

Utterly's dreams now were always of the sea, and of the underneath of the sea. On some nights she dreamed that she saw Sundown Watch as it must appear to strange eyes watching from the waves offshore, with her own self as a tiny doll-like figure in its windows. On others she swam through forests of kelp down into an endless night where ghost-light flickered on the fins of curious fish, and drowned ships hung mouldering in the middle deep. *Utterly*, the sea whispered to her. *Utterly* . . . She usually forgot those dreams as soon as she woke, but the feeling of them remained, like sea salt prickling dry on her skin, and when she knelt on the window seat each evening and watched the horizon, odd fragments of them would come back to her, tickling the edges of her thoughts.

Then one night she dreamed of a beautiful lady who walked out of the waves and stood on the sand, wearing a dress as white as the surf that broke around her feet. When Utterly woke next morning, the dream was so clear in her mind that it felt real.

The lady seemed strangely familiar, and after she had lain for a few minutes turning the dream around in her thoughts, Utterly remembered why. She found a memory of a spring day when she had been very small, perhaps around the time she had learned to breathe underwater in the rock pool. On this day too she had been beach-combing with Mr Dark, and they had turned a corner of the cliffs and seen a lady standing on the shore ahead of them. She had been a long way off, and when he saw her Mr Dark had taken Utterly's hand and said it was time they were going home, and she had gone up the cliff paths with her hand in his and never thought again about the lady till now. But who had she been? And why would she stand there where the little waves were breaking and the salt water was sure to spoil her nice white dress? And was she the same lady who Utterly had just seen in her dream? She had the same black hair, the same pale, solemn face.

Utterly got out of bed and left the house quietly. The garden on the seaward side of Sundown Watch was just a broad stretch of lawn sloping down to a thorn hedge with a gate in it. Beyond the gate a path went by steep zigzags down into Blanchmane's Cove. Utterly stood at the top of the path and looked down. The beach was empty, the tide a long way out. Across the expanse of wet and shining sand long loops and tangles of weed were scattered, looking almost like letters, as if the sea had been trying to scrawl a message there.

Between the weed piles was a line of footprints.

Utterly went down the path. It was steep and muddy, and jagged shards of rock poked out of it like splinters working their way out from an old wound. She had never been down onto the shore except with Mr Dark, and she had always been told not to venture there alone, but she was Watcher now, so it was her duty to try and understand whatever clues the sea had left her.

At the foot of the cliffs she picked her way over the shingle and ran out across the sand to where the footprints were. They had been made by feet that were bigger than hers, but smaller than any grown-up she knew, and they came from the sea. It seemed someone had walked out of the surf just to the edge of the wet sand, and stood there for a while, and then turned and walked back.

Utterly turned her back to the sea, stood in the place where the stranger from the sea had stood, set both her feet in the stranger's footprints, and looked up at the cliffs. She could not see much of Sundown Watch beyond the tops of its chimneys and the semaphore arms on the roof of the Tower. But she distinctly felt someone watching her from behind.

She looked round. The beach was still empty, the waves minding their own business at the mouth of the cove. A few herring gulls were resting on the swell, but Utterly did not think it could be their eyes she had felt upon the back of her neck. She thought of the beautiful lady who had risen from the sea in her dream, and wondered if she might be out there still, hiding in the waves and watching.

'Hello!' she shouted. 'My name is Utterly. What is yours?'

The waves rolled, and the gulls went up and down on them. 'Utterly!' called a voice – but it was only Mrs Skraeveling, up at the house. 'Utterly!'

Utterly turned and ran back up the beach. She made a game of running, but it was not quite a game, because she still had that feeling that something was behind her, watching. She stumbled across clattering pebbles and up the path and did not stop until she reached the clifftop where she turned, breathless, scanning the beach and the far horizon. All she saw were the footprints on the sand: the prints of the stranger's feet coming up to the tide-line, and her own going down to meet them. The waves heaved up green as bottle glass and crumpled into foam. '*Utterly . . .*' they whispered.

'Utterly!' called Mrs Skraeveling, from the kitchen doorway. 'Breakfast!'

❖

'Mrs Skraeveling,' said Utterly, a few slices of toast later. 'Who would go walking on the sand in Blanchmane's Cove?'

'Why, nobody, kitten.'

'Because I saw footprints there.'

Mrs Skraeveling shook her head. 'You should not go down to the beach, Utterly.'

'But the tide was far out, I was perfectly safe.'

'There is no such thing as perfectly safe where the sea is concerned,' said Mrs Skraeveling, pouring more tea. She looked along the table at her husband. 'Skraeveling, you don't think that old sea-witch might have come walking in our cove?'

'Not unless she swam there,' said Mr Skraeveling. 'No, I don't reckon old Thurza Froy strays far from her lair these days. I expect those were birds' prints you saw on the sand, kitten.'

Utterly knew they had not been, but she did not try to explain. She was thinking about the sea-witch. Thurza Froy must know something of the Hidden Lands. Perhaps she had seen them too, the night of the storm, when she had lit her fire on the Undercliff. As Watcher, it was Utterly's duty to question her. If something was stirring out there on the sea, a sea-witch was just the person to ask about it.

The idea was almost as daunting as the idea of going to talk to Aish, but not quite, because while Thurza Froy might be a witch, at least she was not a troll as well. Besides, the Undercliff was not nearly such a long walk as the Dizzard. And best of all, Utterly would not have to go there alone.

After she had done her chores and the Skraevelings were busy with their own, Utterly put on her bonnet and walked down the cliff track to Marazea. It was washday at the vicarage, and Mrs Dearlove and her children were helping their maid peg out the laundry.

'Mrs Dearlove,' said Utterly. 'When you take a pot of jam to Thurza Froy, I would like to come with you, if I may.'

'Would you, my dear?' asked Mrs Dearlove, blinking at her over a pile of damp bedsheets.

'Yes. I see her fires from my bedroom window sometimes,' Utterly explained. 'I think she must be very lonely down there.'

'I believe she is,' said Mrs Dearlove sadly. 'And I am afraid the solitude has made her somewhat eccentric. It is very kind and Christian of you to think of her, Utterly.'

'When will you go to see her?' asked Utterly. 'I should like to go today, if possible.'

'It is a duty I tend to put off,' said Mrs Dearlove. 'Mrs Froy is – well, not always the most agreeable company. But you are right, my dear, it is high time I went to see her, and this is a lovely day for a walk. Why don't you help Lucy fold these sheets, while I gather the jam and some other things in a basket, and then we shall go down to the Undercliff together.'

14

THE LEGEND OF THURZA FROY

The sea-witch was not a Wildsea woman, but the daughter of a boat-builder from Finnery. She had been a pretty girl once, and skilled in her father's trade, and a handsome Merriport fisherman named Davey Froy had thought her a prize catch when he brought her home with him to be his wife. But Thurza had a bright and clever mind, and that was the last thing a Merriport fish-wife needed. Once the first shine of newness had worn off her marriage, she started to grow restless in Davey's neat little cottage. It was then that her thoughts had first started to turn to the legends of the Gorm.

Finnery lay far to the east of Wildsea, and such stories of the Hidden Lands as Thurza had heard when she was growing up were more about their mystery and promise than their terror. Lost sailors were said to have glimpsed ruined palaces on their shores, with roofs of gold and floors of ivory which would have made them the richest men in Christendom if they'd only had time to land and prise up a tile or two – but, of course, the sailors in the stories never did, and they were never able to find the Hidden Lands again, however hard they looked.

'But if you could find them, Davey-boy,' Thurza told her husband, 'you could have their treasures for yourself. Then think how rich we'd be! Then there would be no more need for you to go out at all hours upon the restless sea, chasing the elusive herring and the wily sprat. We could build us a big house up on the clifftop there, and look down our noses at everyone in Merriport.'

'Don't be daft, woman,' scoffed Davey Froy. 'Everybody knows the Hidden Lands show up only when they feel like it. If them old sailors never found 'em again, how in blue blazes do you think I could?'

'Because them old sailors lived in an age of ignorance and superstition,' said Thurza. 'But you live in an age of reason, Davey-boy. It stands to reason islands don't just vanish. They *sank*, that's what happened. And they are hidden down beneath the wild waves still, and not too deep, most likely, since they gets lifted up from time to time by an undersea volcano or some other natural marvel of that sort. The men of olden times could not get to them. But men nowadays have worked out a means for descending into the sea.'

And she told Davey about a gentleman from Edinburgh who had arrived on Finnery with a diving suit, and walked around in it at the bottom of the harbour to fetch up salvage from a sunken ship.

'I would look a proper fool in one of those,' said Davey Froy, when she described the suit to him. But the gleam of lost treasure had found its way from Thurza's mind into his own. From then on, whenever he was hauling in nets of silvery herring, he would think how much finer it would be to haul in nets of actual silver. The golden roofs of Thurza's story gleamed always just beneath the surface of his thoughts, just as the roofs themselves must gleam, a few fathoms beneath the surface of the western sea.

At last he said, 'Very well – let's find those Hidden Lands, and see what treasures lie there.'

So Thurza took her sailmaker's needles and set about making him a diving suit. She made it from sealskins, rubbing tallow and mutton fat into them to make them supple and waterproof, and sealing the seams with tar. It was a baggy, saggy sort of suit, with a mitten stitched to the end of each arm, and lead-soled boots on the ends of the legs. Instead of a hat it had a great conical hood stretched over a wicker frame. Two small circular windows in the front of the hood shone as coldly as the eyes of sharks, and from the back of it a sheep-gut tube uncoiled for ten fathoms, so that Davey would still be able to breathe the good air of the world above.

Davey and Thurza tested the suit in secret, in one of the coves of the south coast, in case anyone worked out what they were about.

"'Tis like a beautiful garden down there, Thurza girl,' said Davey, as he came staggering out of the surf. When he took off that sinister hood he looked moonstruck and unlike himself, as if he'd seen a vision. 'All that old kelp do swirl about on the tide like an invisible wind be blowing it. Starryfish shine out like flowers on lawns of underwater grass. 'Tis the Garden of Eden down there, maybe . . .'

Now it was Thurza's turn to tell Davey *he* was daft. It was good solid gold they were hunting, not invisible winds and poetical undersea gardens. But the trial had worked. The suit was watertight. They were ready to begin their quest.

They set out aboard Davey's fishing boat a few days later. There were only the two of them aboard, for Thurza reasoned that if they brought any of Davey's shipmates with them they would have to share the treasure, and why should she consent to that, when all the hard work had been hers alone? She was all the crew her Davey needed.

The Watcher of the time, Will and Andrewe's grandfather Jeremiah Dark, saw them from the lawns of

Sundown Watch and made an entry about it in the Log: *Around 9 a.m, the Weather being Fair and the Wind from the south-east, a Merriport Lugger rounded Gull Point. We did fire off Guns, and shouted till our Faces was Blue, trying to warn her Master of his Folly, but he did not hear us, and the Vessel was last seen making west. May God have mercy upon them.*

That was the last anyone on Wildsea ever heard of Davey Froy. That afternoon a squall blew up, and next day Thurza was washed ashore on the beaches of the Undercliff, bitter, battered and alone. There she had lived ever since, lighting her driftwood fires, chanting her spells, cursing and envying and worshipping the Gorm. Wildsea folk said she could heal warts. They said she could brew up love potions. They whispered that, in exchange for gifts of gin, or nails, or sailcloth, she would ask the Gorm to drown your faithless husband or your nagging wife.

15

JAM FOR THE SEA-WITCH

Long ago the stretch of cliffs just north of Marazea had sunk to its knees to form the Undercliff, a hummocked, boulder-strewn shelf of land halfway between the surf and the new clifftops behind it. Few people ventured there, and nature had made a jungle of it.

Only animal paths led through the tangled thickets of gorse and small trees. While Mrs Dearlove made her way carefully along them with the basket of provisions for Thurza Froy, the children hurried ahead of her like the advance guard of a small invasion force. To their right the cliff face rose up steeply. To their left it fell away just as steeply, and they could hear the boom of breakers on the shore below, but the vegetation was so thick they caught only glimpses of the sea.

'We're going to see the sea-witch!' they sang, until Mrs Dearlove had to remind them that there were no such things as witches. After that, Horatio amused himself by slashing at the brambles with his wooden cutlass, while Utterly and the girls picked blackberries. At least half the blackberries were sour, because after Michaelmas the Devil widdled on them, but that did not stop them trying more, until their hands and mouths were purple with the juice.

The sea-witch must have been able to hear them coming for a full half-hour before they finally emerged onto the scruffy promontory where her shack stood, but there was no sign of life there. The witch's fireplace was a circle of blackened earth. The shack itself looked as if the sea might have made it by heaping driftwood randomly against a few big rocks. All around, like sentries, ugly totems made of stacked-up boulders stood, fluttering scraps of fishing net for hair.

'Mrs Froy!' trilled Mrs Dearlove. She tapped politely on the sea-witch's front door as if it really were a door and not just a fragment of shipwreck lashed with rope hinges to an upright post. Utterly and the other children gathered behind her, wide-eyed and giggly. Lucy squeaked with excitement when the door opened an inch.

A bird-bright eye peered at them from the shadows. Mrs Dearlove held out her basket. 'Here is a fruit-loaf, some pears, a cabbage from the kitchen garden, and a pot of this year's raspberry jam, with all our compliments,' she said.

Thurza Froy bared long yellow teeth. 'I don't need your scraps, Lady Bountiful,' she snarled. 'The sea looks after its own. Good fresh fish it gives to me.'

'You cannot live by fish alone,' said Mrs Dearlove.

'And crabs. And mussels. And kelp,' the witch went on, but she opened the door wider and snatched the basket. The daylight fell upon her cobweb hair and hairy, wizened face. She scowled at the children.

'You remember my little ones,' Mrs Dearlove told her helpfully.

The old woman glanced at the Dearlove children without interest. Then her attention settled on Utterly, and Utterly was not altogether sure she welcomed it. There was something a bit shivery-making about the way those beady black eyes regarded her.

'You look like *her*,' the sea-witch said.

'Like who, Mrs Froy?' asked Utterly.

But the old woman shut her mouth tight, as if those words had escaped without her meaning them to, and she was making sure no more could follow them.

'This is Utterly Dark, from Sundown Watch,' said Mrs Dearlove sunnily. 'It was Utterly who suggested we should come and call on you today.'

'I have often seen your fires, Mrs Froy,' said Utterly.

The sea-witch spat at her, or at least made a spitting

sound – there seemed to be no spittle in her dry old mouth. 'And do you know why I lights 'em? It is to call the Gorm so it shall come and trample you all, and cause the sea to rise up and drown you. 'Twill not be long now! The Hidden Lands have shown themselves again. Now the Gorm shall come, and you'll be trampled flat and drownded deep, girl, and this simpering cow and all her brood too, and that smug husband of hers, and all the other fine fools o' this cursed island.'

'But aren't you worried about being trampled and drowned yourself?' asked Utterly, ignoring Mrs Dearlove, who was saying briskly, 'Well, my dears, I think we really should be going,' and gently trying to draw Utterly away.

The sea-witch made her spitting sound again. 'Trampled? Drownded? Not I! Not Thurza Froy! I have built myself a boat such as will carry me safe over the waves while you proud hooligans gurgle and gargle and go down smothering beneath them. Oh, you shall reach out your pretty hands to old Thurza for to save you, but will I have pity on you? Not I! Gorm take 'ee, I shall say, and while it is busy trampling you I shall sail away to the Hidden Lands, and claim their treasures for my own, and there my Davey will be waiting for me.'

'Dear Thurza,' said Mrs Dearlove, 'your Davey was drowned, do you recall? He waits for you in Heaven, not the Hidden Lands.'

'He waits in the Hidden Lands!' the sea-witch snarled. 'Drowning don't mean nothing there, for the drowned may walk if the Gorm wills it. I'll go to him, and he will know me, and we shall laugh together thinking of your corpses a-bloating in the great deep like turds in a chamber pot.'

'Mama! She said "turds"!' hissed Lucy, deliciously scandalized.

'Now, children,' said Mrs Dearlove, with the air of one who felt things were getting a little out of hand. 'We must not trouble Mrs Froy any longer. And Mrs Froy, I hope you know in your heart that there is one far greater than the Gorm. It is with His love that we brought you our little gifts . . .'

'You mean little baby Jesus?' cackled the old woman. 'Gentle Jesus, meek and mild? I called *his* name when the sea came for my Davey, and much good it did either of us. The sea was here before your God, and it will be here after. *He* don't have no power to command it.'

'Come, children,' said Mrs Dearlove in a voice full of false cheerfulness, and turned away, calling them to follow.

But as Utterly went after the others, the sea-witch suddenly darted out of her shack and caught her by the arm. 'Girl,' she said, and her voice was falsely cheerful too, or trying to be. It was as if she realized her rudeness had driven the visitors away, and she was trying too late to make amends. She bared her teeth in a simpering smile and said, 'Pretty miss, won't you take pity on old Thurza? Won't you unlock the gate of Sundown Watch for me, so I may creep out onto the Gorm's Head and make a fire? Just the littlest of fires, to warm my old bones by?'

Gorm's Head was an old name for St Chyan's Head, where the stone circle stood. Sundown Watch and its wall and ditch had been built specifically to stop people like Thurza lighting fires there. Utterly flinched free of the old woman's grasp and said, 'I am sorry, I cannot do that.'

The witch's smile, which had never been very convincing, dropped off her face like a picture falling off a wall. 'Gorm take 'ee, then,' she snarled. 'I shall light my beacons where I may, and one night it will see me. It will not be long now. Already I have seen Men o' Weed walking. The Gorm itself will not be far behind.'

She darted back into her shack and slammed the door, shaking the whole rickety structure. Utterly ran to catch up with the Dearloves. 'You must understand,' Mrs Dearlove was saying, 'that poor Mrs Froy believes in things that can never be. But it is our Christian duty to show her kindness all the same.'

Lucy and Horatio ran on ahead. They were already forgetting about the sea-witch, but Utterly hung back with their mother and little Emily. The Hidden Lands have begun to show themselves again, she thought. And she wondered whether the drowned could really walk if the Gorm willed it, and if their dead feet would leave footprints in the sand of Blanchmane's Cove, and what on earth the Men o' Weed might be.

16

AT THE WINDOW

By the time Utterly got home that afternoon the tide was on its way out again. Before dinner she sneaked down into Blanchmane's Cove, but there were no footprints on the sand, and she no longer felt the sea's eyes upon her. She thought again of the lady from her dream, and wondered if she came every night to stand where the waves broke and look up at the cliffs. If only she would climb the path to the clifftop, Utterly would be able to see her. If only she would come and knock at the door, Utterly would be able to ask her about the Hidden Lands and the Gorm; she was sure to know far more about them than old Thurza Froy.

Utterly went right to the sea's edge, crouched down, and drew her initials in the wet sand, and then an arrow pointing to the path that led up the cliff. She regretted it almost at once, and was about to scuff the marks out when a little wave came rushing in so fast that she had to skip backwards to stop her shoes from being damped. Foam filled up the lines she had drawn, and when the wave drew back the sand was smooth again. The sea had read her message, the same way she and Lucy Dearlove read the inscriptions on the oldest stones in the churchyard by running their fingers over the faint letters.

Utterly stood on the tideline and waited nervously for a reply, but nothing happened, and the Hidden Lands did not spring into being on the horizon. Feeling a little disappointed, she hurried back up the cliff to change and set the dinner table.

But perhaps the sea had been paying attention after all, for later that evening when she was keeping her private Watch she finally did see something.

It was after sundown. She had heard Uncle Will's footsteps on the stairs as he came down from his Watch in the Tower, and she was taking one last look at the sea before she went to bed. The sea and sky were all one twilight-grey that night, except high overhead where the sun's last rays were pinking the feathered edges of frail little clouds. Utterly was about to turn away when, out at the mouth of Blanchmane's Cove, something round and dark broke the surface of the sea. It was the size of a head, but it was not altogether the *shape* of a head. As Utterly

101

peered at it, trying to make out whether it was floating on the surface or just the upper part of some larger, submerged thing, it suddenly turned towards her, and even from that distance she saw the quick glint of its eyes.

Startled, Utterly jerked back from the window. Whatever it was out there, it was not the smiling lady from her dream. *Perhaps it was a seal,* she told herself. But everyone knew there were no seals around the western shores of Wildsea. Seals had more sense than to pursue their sealy business in that haunted ocean.

Holding her breath, she put her face to the window again. The head was gone, the cove deserted. 'I imagined it,' she said, and felt suddenly more inclined to accept Uncle Will's sensible, comforting belief that things you thought you saw weren't always there.

She closed the shutters and undressed, scrubbed her face quickly and not very well at the washstand, put on her nightdress, and climbed into bed. But when she had snuffed the candle and settled down to sleep, an unsettling thought crept into her head and would not leave . . .

What if the thing she had seen had disappeared, not because she'd imagined it, or because it had sunk back into the sea, but *because it had swum closer to the shore*, where it would be hidden from her by the cliffs?

Utterly imagined it slipping and slithering its way up the beach, up the steep cliff path, over the lawns towards the house, following the arrow she had so foolishly drawn in the sand. What it was exactly, she could not have said. The Gorm itself, all fangs and fish scales, like the painting in the living room? A drowned mariner drawn to the warmth of the lamplight showing through the heart-shaped holes in the drawing room shutters? Dead Davey Froy himself in his appalling sealskin suit? Utterly did not know. She only knew that she could not sleep until she had proven to herself that there was nothing there.

She threw the coverlets off and padded over to the window, finding her way easily enough in the dark, feeling for the brass catch on the shutters, undoing it, swinging them open. The moon was surprisingly bright. At first all Utterly could see was her own face reflected in the glass, pale and indistinct, like a girl made of mist. Then slowly, and with a gathering horror, she realized that there was another face on the far side of the glass, looking in at her.

It was not a human face. It was a mockery of one made out of seaweed; a glistening, ragged, roughly face-shaped mass of wet kelp and bladderwrack, and it was watching Utterly with eyes that were two cold, unblinking shards of sea-smoothed glass.

❖

Utterly felt as though she had been screaming for a long time before the grown-ups came; first Mrs Skraeveling asking, 'What is it, kitten? What is it, Utterly my love?' Then Uncle Will, wondering what all the racket was about, and finally, when she had sobbingly explained about *the face, the face, all made of seaweed*, Mr Skraeveling, barefoot, with a coat slung on over his nightshirt and his old blunderbuss pistol in his hands, who led Uncle Will outside to search for the intruder.

Utterly stayed close to Mrs Skraeveling in the fan of lamplight from the open back door while the men marched around the garden shouting importantly, 'Hallo? Hallo! Who's there? Show yourself!' After a while, when no one answered, they came back to the house, looking embarrassed now by Mr Skraeveling's gun and the ash stick that Uncle Will had snatched from the hall stand.

'A bad dream is all it was, I expect,' said Mrs Skraeveling.

'But it was not a dream! I was *awake*,' insisted Utterly. 'I was wide awake, and I *saw* it. It was a Man o' Weed!'

'And whatever is a Man o' Weed when he's at home?' asked Uncle Will.

Mr Skraeveling frowned. 'They're just a name folks give to tangles of seaweed they find cast up in odd places sometimes. They are man-sized and sometimes sort of man-shaped, and if they are too far from the shore we call 'em Men o' Weed and say they must have walked there.'

'Thurza Froy told us about them when I was down on the Undercliff with the Dearloves,' said Utterly.

'The old sea-witch?' Uncle Will sounded surprised.

'You don't want to be a-listening to that mad old woman, Utterly,' said Mr Skraeveling.

'But she was *right!*' insisted Utterly. 'The Men o' Weed will walk, she said, and now a Man o' Weed *has* walked – he has walked right up to my window, and looked in at me!'

'Nonsense, kitten,' said Mrs Skraeveling. But Uncle Will – perhaps remembering how he had accused Utterly of imagining the Hidden Lands, and not wishing to accuse her a second time of inventing things, said, 'Well, we have frightened him away, whatever he may have been. And anything that may be frightened away by me and Mr Skraeveling cannot be so very terrible, can it?'

'Or perhaps it was an owl?' said Mrs Skraeveling helpfully.

'Can Utterly sleep with you tonight?' asked Uncle Will. It was exactly what Utterly had been wanting to ask but had not quite liked to. Uncle Will smiled at her and said, 'When I was your age I was somewhat prone to nightmares, and I always found it a great comfort to make a little nest of blankets in Mr and Mrs Skraeveling's room, and sleep in there.'

Utterly was so surprised by his understanding that she could not answer, except to nod her head. She decided that she liked her uncle a little better than she had thought.

Mr Skraeveling went to take a last look round the gardens with the slightly wistful air of a man who has loaded a gun and found no excuse to let it off. Mrs Skraeveling said, 'Come along then, kitten, let's find some blankets for your nest.'

17

THE DIZZARD

Utterly slept dreamlessly that night, snug as a sleepy dog in her nest of quilts and coverlets on the Skraevelings' bedroom floor. She woke at first light when they got up to start their morning chores, and returned to her own room to find nothing but daylight peeking through the shutters.

Dressing quickly, she went outside. The early morning air was cold and bright, and white breakers were rolling shoreward on a west wind, filling the gardens with their steady roar. Utterly walked along the seaward side of the house and looked at the bare flowerbed under her bedroom window. She was not sure what she expected to see there. Footprints? The soil was trampled-looking, it was true, but it had probably been trampled by Uncle Will and Mr Skraeveling.

Something showed pale in the dark earth, and she stooped to peer more closely at it. It was a small dead crab lying on its back, like a tiny, intricately-jointed gauntlet made from white porcelain. Well, Utterly thought, things must often be blown ashore, when the wind is from the west like this. But the garden was high above the sea, and she had never noticed crabs in it before. She turned and looked around, and saw that there was a trail of seaweed scattered across the lawn. Not very much of it, just stray strands and straggles that might have gone unnoticed in the light of Uncle Will's lantern the previous night, but definitely a trail. She followed it down the slope of the lawn to the gate in the hedge, and found a flag of seaweed hanging there. Beyond the gate there were more scraps of weed strewn on the path down to Blanchmane's Cove. At the cliff's foot a big tangle of seaweed was lying on the stones. It did not look quite like a man, but it did not look quite *unlike* a man.

Utterly stared down at it for a long time. If something *had* been looking in at her window, and if it had fled when she started screaming, and lost its footing as it ran down the cliff path, then that was the very place it would have fallen. She could not see from up on the clifftop if it had two sea-glass eyes, and she was afraid to go down and take a closer look, in case it did. She toyed with the idea of running to fetch Mr Skraeveling or Uncle Will, but the tide was coming in quickly. She watched as the boisterous waves jostled and worried the pile, lifted it, and dragged it out to become part of the great cold salad of torn weed which the sea was tossing in the cove.

It does not matter anyway, she thought. They would only say it was nothing but sea-wrack. Uncle Will had been surprisingly nice after she saw the Man o' Weed, but she could tell he had not believed in it any more than Mr and Mrs Skraeveling had. She needed to tell someone who actually understood such things.

For a moment she almost considered going back to the Undercliff and seeking out Thurza Froy. Then she remembered Aish telling her, *You come and find me if you see things stirring.* As if Aish had almost been expecting things to stir. As if she would know what to do about them when they did. At the time, Utterly had not imagined ever accepting her invitation, but now that she had faced a sea-witch and a Man o' Weed, paying calls on trolls did not seem quite such a daunting prospect.

She looked north along the coast to where the tree-clad hills of the Dizzard rose out of the morning mist. Mr Skraeveling had said it was a half-day's walk, so she reckoned that if she started now she might be there by noon, and back home again in time for supper. She would need to take provisions for herself, and a gift for Aish too, because it was rude to call on someone empty-handed. She would ask Mrs Skraeveling if she could take the remaining half of that prodigious great cake that was in the pantry. But she would not tell Mrs Skraeveling she was going to the Dizzard; she would say that she was visiting the Dearloves, and that the cake was for them.

She hurried back up the lawn to the house, making her plans as she went. Behind her, the waves filled Blanchmane's Cove, rushing up white between the rocks and falling back and rushing up again like white hands clawing and clawing at the land.

❖

A half-day's walk, Mr Skraeveling had said, but his legs were longer and stronger than Utterly's, or maybe he had been misremembering. Beyond Marazea the coast path led behind the Undercliff and on over a switchback of steep cliffs. Utterly plodded along it for the whole morning with her heavy knapsack banging against her side. The October sun was hot and bright, but the wind was blowing puffball clouds in from the sea, and each time their shadows fell across her she felt the breath of winter in the air.

By midday she had only gone as far as the old hill fort at Trollbrook Mouth. There she rested on one of the grassy ramparts and ate a piece of Mrs Skraeveling's cake. She wondered if she should give up her expedition, but she had come so far it seemed a shame to turn back now. So she ate a second piece of cake to make her knapsack lighter, and set off again.

Beyond the fort the road turned inland along the bank of the Trollbrook, a fast, busy, chuckling sort of river full of the brown, peaty water which poured out of the upland bogs as if from a squeezed sponge. On its far bank the rocky hills of the Dizzard rose steeply, covered with trees whose autumn leaves shimmered with gold in each gust from the sea. Utterly could see no sign of trolls at all. She crossed the packhorse bridge below the inn at Trollbridge and followed a steep path uphill through the trees, over shelves of mossy stone which looked like stairs. She thought they might have been stairs once, long ago, before the moss and the tree roots and the thick layers of leaf mould covered them.

'Aish!' she shouted, and waited nervously for trolls to leap out of the bushes and grab her, or drop a weighted net on her as if she was a bird. But only the trees moved, and all she heard was the echoes of her own voice go bounding away across the steep slopes.

The Dizzard was nothing like the rest of Wildsea. The hillside was scattered with huge boulders, all furred with deep green moss. Between the boulders grew the ancient trees, their bark grey with stone-coloured lichen. It was a confusing, in-betweeny place where the rocks seemed to be turning into trees, the trees into rocks.

'Aish!' Utterly shouted. 'Miss Aish!'

Birds flapped from the branches. She climbed on, through dappled light and shifting shadows, stopping sometimes to shout Aish's name. She heard no answer to her calls, and saw no trolls, but sometimes she saw the signs that trolls had been about: a talisman of twigs and hair dangling from a branch beside the path; a cow's skull tied to the bole of an old oak; a wicker fish-trap wedged between the rocks of a stream. She did not see the boy who was watching her until he called out, 'Hey!'

He was squatting in the fork of an oak above the path. He seemed about the same age as Utterly, but smaller and stockier. He did not look like a troll. His face was freckled and cheeky beneath a tussock of rusty hair. 'You are the girl from Sundown Watch,' he said.

'I am,' Utterly admitted, hoping to hide how much he had startled her.

The boy jumped down from his perch, came close to Utterly, stared into her face, then reached out and fingered the sleeve of her dress as if he was wondering what it was made from. His own clothing ran only to a pair of patched breeches and a spear with a blade of greenish stone which hung on his back from a strap he wore across his chest. The cattle he had been watching nibbled the grass between the trees, as stocky and rusty-red as himself.

'If you've finished peering at me,' said Utterly, 'I've come to see Aish. On Watcher's business.'

'She's up yonder,' said the boy. 'Which she heard you hollerin', and sent me for to fetch you.' He grinned, and set off scrambling up a path so narrow that Utterly had not noticed it till then, and so steep that she needed both hands and all her wits to follow him.

She emerged from the trees at last onto a high rocky place where a stone had been set upright. Old carvings showed beneath its flocking of lichen; circles within circles within circles. Beyond the stone the land dropped away and away down dizzying tree-clad steeps to the sea. Catching sight of the sea again after so long in the woods was a relief, thought Utterly; like taking a deep gulp of air when you had been holding your breath for a while. It was blue in the afternoon sun, and covered with mysterious wandering ribbons of smooth water paler than the rest, like roads winding to nowhere.

Aish sat by the stone, looking out over the sea, so still that Utterly thought at first she might be praying to the old gods of the place. But the boy, who had run ahead of Utterly and scrambled up onto a rock to wait for her, said loudly, 'Aish, that girl is here.'

The troll-woman had left off her antlers, and put on instead the curly horns of a ram. She did not turn to look at Utterly. She pointed to the sea. 'Look! Dragons!'

Utterly shielded her eyes against the sunlight. A short way offshore the waves were breaking over a vicious reef called the Knacker's Knife-rack. Just beyond it Utterly saw a slender neck lift from the water, arching like the neck of a black swan. She wished she had brought the Watcher's telescope with her. From this distance she could not make out the rows of needle-sharp teeth, the distinctive seahorse crests and trailing barbels. Still, it was a thrill to see a real, live sea dragon, not just an engraving in a book. Another rose, and the two beasts seemed to bow to one another like dancers.

'They are busy courting,' said Aish.

'I've never seen sea dragons before,' said Utterly. 'Lucy Dearlove says she saw one once, but I think she was fibbing.'

Aish nodded solemnly, as if she knew all about Lucy and thought it more than likely. 'They often play out there where the white water is,' she said. 'Look, he is stretching up his great long neck to let her see how strong and beautiful he is, the big show-off, and she is deciding whether she will have him for her sweetheart. I came up here hoping for a sight of them and there they are. And here you are. So this is a good day. You are as welcome as the flowers in May.'

Utterly remembered her manners. 'I brought you a cake, Miss Aish,' she said, fetching it out of her knapsack. 'I'm afraid it has got somewhat squashed, and quite a lot of it has been eaten, but it has icing, and sugared almonds.'

'It is a very fine cake,' said Aish, and took out a clasp-knife to cut it into three pieces, one for herself, one for Utterly, and one for the boy. When she had eaten her piece, and licked the last of the icing from her fingers, she said, 'And now tell me all you have seen, Watcher.'

'I saw the islands,' said Utterly. 'It was the night before the storm. But I am not Watcher any more, because my uncle Will has come home, so he is Watcher now. Only he did not believe me about the islands. I do not think he believes in the Hidden Lands at all, nor the Gorm, nor any of it.'

Aish shook her head in a way that showed she was disappointed but not much surprised. 'Your uncle Will is a fool then,' she said.

Utterly laughed, but then felt a little ashamed of herself. 'He was very kind to me last night, when I was frightened,' she admitted.

'And what had frightened you, Utterly Dark?' asked Aish, as if she already knew.

'Have you ever seen a thing like a man made of weed?' said Utterly. 'Kelp and bladderwrack all tangled up, with glass for eyes? It walks about and peeps in people's windows.'

For a moment she thought that Aish was frightened too. Her eyes widened, and she stiffened, and her nostrils flared, and she put up one hand to the charms around her neck. Then the moment passed, and she looked calm again, but very serious. She said, 'You have seen such a creature?'

Utterly told her what had occurred at Sundown

Watch. 'And Thurza Froy said Men o' Weed would walk and then the Gorm would come . . .'

'The sea washed old Thurza's wits away long since,' said Aish. 'But the Gorm is stirring. I can feel her out there, when the wind is from the west. I have felt her often these past weeks. It is like the feeling that comes before a storm.'

'I feel it too,' said Utterly. 'Not like a storm, but – I feel as if the sea is watching me.' She shivered. The sun had moved behind the rocks on the hill top, and the air was suddenly cold. She jumped to her feet and reached for her knapsack. 'I must go!' she said. 'I will be late for dinner, and Mrs Skraeveling will be worrying . . .'

Aish stood up too. 'No,' she said. 'It will be dark long before you reach home, and dangerous with those weed-dollies wandering. You must stay safe here tonight. Tomorrow I shall walk back with you, and we shall have a word with this foolish uncle of yours.'

18

AISH'S LOOKOUT

Utterly had never spent a night away from Sundown Watch before, at least not since she was a baby in a seaborne basket. She knew Mr and Mrs Skraeveling would be fretting about her. But the sun was already quite low in the west, and she did not like the thought of walking home in the dark, past all those lonely coves where whole gangs of weed-men might be lying in wait. Besides, she was intrigued to see whether the Dizzard people really lived in caves, as Mrs Skraeveling had once claimed.

Aish set off briskly up the hill, walking the same way she talked; quickly, and with no sign that she realized Utterly was any littler than her. Utterly hurried after her, and the boy kept her company, although he said he could have gone much faster if he had wanted to, and sometimes ran ahead to prove it and climbed another tree or rock to wait for Utterly to catch up. He was annoying, but Utterly was glad of him, for Aish was out of sight ahead somewhere. Only her voice could be heard sometimes, singing among the trees.

'What is your spear for?' Utterly asked the boy.

'Rabbits,' he said. 'Foxes. Wolves. It's good and sharp. I made it myself.'

'There aren't any wolves on Wildsea,' Utterly told him. 'I don't think there are even any left in England.'

'Well, if one swims here from somewhere else, I'll be ready for it,' said the boy, reaching over his shoulder to touch his spear. 'I ain't afraid of a wolf.'

'Is Aish your mother?'

'No!'

'Your sister then?'

'Course not.'

'What's your name?'

'Egg,' said the boy.

'What sort of name is Egg?'

'What sort is Utterly?'

'Is Aish your auntie then?'

'She ain't no kind of relation to me at all,' said Egg.

'Then you are her servant boy?'

Egg laughed at that. He climbed on ahead a way and then stopped and waited for Utterly to catch up with him and said, 'My people come from Merriport. But my mum died when I was little and my dad was a ruffian who spent all his wages on liquor and beat me when it was gone. So I run off, didn't I?'

It was a sadder answer than Utterly had expected. So that was why he had not wanted to tell her about himself. She was sorry that she had asked him now.

'I lived for a while on the beaches over Stack Head way,' said Egg. 'Birds nest on the sea cliffs there and you can take their eggs easy if you ain't scared of heights. I ain't scared of heights. I ain't scared of anything really. But then winter come and the wind turned easterly and I found my way up here to this old Dizzard looking for shelter from it. I made a nest among the rocks, and took to stealing chickens and loaves of bread and whatever else the trolls left out unwatched. I was clever at it too,' he added proudly. 'They never spotted me. They thought I was a ghost. But Aish is cleverer even than me. She tracked me to my hidey-hole and said wouldn't I rather work for my dinner instead of pinching it, and sleep by her hearth instead of under a cold old stone. And I thought about it and decided, and I've been at her place ever since. We suit each other pretty well. I go errands for her sometimes, as a favour, but don't you go thinking I'm her servant. Aish is my friend, and I am hers.'

Utterly, who had felt very sorry for him when he spoke about his dead mother and his cruel dad, now suddenly found herself envying him. There was no adult she could have called a friend, exactly. It made Egg seem much more grown-up than her.

They went on in silence. The path grew steep again, winding up through a gap in a tumbled, mossy wall and out into an open place above, where Utterly smelled the smoke of fires, and good things cooking. She looked around, wondering if the crags and grassy knolls that covered the hilltop held the caves in which the trolls lived.

But Mrs Skraeveling had been misinformed – the troll-houses were not caves but little cottages. Their roofs were covered with turf and grass, which is what had made them seem like knolls at first, and most of them were built against the craggy outcrops, using the living rock as part of their walls. Goats and chickens milled about. Amiable dogs wandered over to sniff Utterly. Children came running to stare at her. Grown-ups watched her from cottage doorways, and called out greetings to Aish. Apart from their shaggy hair and old-fashioned clothes most of them looked much like people in Marazea or Stack. Few were as trollish as Aish. Perhaps that was why they seemed to treat her as a person of some importance, bobbing their heads respectfully as she went by, just as Marazea people did if they met the Watcher. Utterly started to feel rather proud to be in Aish's company.

'This is Dizzard Tor,' said Aish. 'There are dozens of farms and villages tucked into the nooks and crannies of the Dizzard, but this is the biggest. It is where people first settled when they came to Wildsea. They did not know they were on an island then, because the world was so cold in those days that the sea had frozen right across, and snow lay deep upon the ice, and islands stuck up from it like white mountains rising from a white plain. They walked from one to another of them until they reached this hill, and climbed it, and made their homes up here. It was a shock when finally the snow melted and the ice broke up and they found sea all around them. And more of a shock when they realized the sea wasn't empty, and the old Gorm was out there watching them. Still, I am glad they came. It was lonely before.'

She spoke as if she remembered the trolls' arrival, which was puzzling, because Utterly felt sure the sea had not frozen right across in living memory, and perhaps not since before the Flood.

She did not have time to wonder about it though. Aish led her inside her own house, which was set a little apart from the rest, and most of the village crowded in behind her, bringing food to share, and watching Utterly curiously while she ate. She thought she would feel shy among so many strangers, but everyone seemed friendly. She was introduced to lots of people, young and old, whose names and relationships to one another she forgot almost at once. It was very confusing, and easier just to eat the food Aish set in front of her and listen

121

to the trolls' soft, flowing speech, which broke often and often into song. There was bread almost as good as Mrs Skraeveling's, with rich yellow butter soaking into it, beef stew with dumplings, then baked apples, dragged sizzling from the ashes in the fireplace and drizzled with cream. Egg, who seemed to have decided he was Utterly's protector, made sure she got two of those.

When she had eaten, Aish turned to her and said, 'Now come. The old sun is on his way to bed, and we should take a look at the sea before he pulls the covers over and starts to snore.'

Utterly went with her gladly. She could not remember why she had ever been scared of Aish. There *was* something wild about her, but it was a wildness like the wildness of the sea – the thrilling sort, not the frightening sort.

A spiralling path led up the last steep crag above the village, turning into stairs as it neared the summit. On the very top, a natural basin in the granite cupped a trembling pool. Utterly stood beside it and looked out, and saw the Dizzard woods below her, and the last light gleaming on a lake between the trees, and beyond the trees the deep blue evening sea. She had almost forgotten about the sea while she had been in the woods and in Aish's home, and seeing all it all around her surprised her almost as much as it must once have surprised the trolls.

'I told you I keep my own watch for the Hidden Lands,' said Aish. 'Not every night, but always at the hinges of the year. Magic is an in-between thing. It happens in the halfway places, between day and night, land and sea, man and woman, one season and the next. Midwinter, midsummer, spring-fire and autumn. That is when the Hidden Lands draw closest to our world. That is when I watch for them and this is where I watch from. The name of this rock is called Aish's Lookout.'

They sat beside the pool and watched the daylight fade. In the north and the east Utterly could see dozens of islands, but they were the ordinary sort of islands which stayed where God had put them and whose names she knew from the *Atlas of the Autumn Isles* in the book-case at Sundown Watch. She could make out Hoyt with all its harbour lights, the low dark wedge of Finnery, and Seapitts under its fug of quarry smoke. But to the west the sea was empty, as if Wildsea really did sit at the edge of the world.

'Way back-along,' said Aish, 'when the people who came here across the ice had got used to living here, they began to notice the Hidden Lands. Seen across the sea at sundown they looked like fine country, better than Wildsea. They began to make offerings to the Gorm, in the hope that she would come and take them to her islands. They set standing stones upon the headland and lit fires for her. And the Gorm was flattered. She came to

123

the sea's edge as a pretty woman, and grew tipsy on their love and worship, for she is a vain old thing.

'But she is temperamental too, and somehow they offended her – did not bow low enough perhaps, or lit too small a fire – so she put on a more monstrous form and came storming and raging to sweep them all into the deep. All their towns were washed away, and half my woods too.' Aish shook her head. 'I told them it was a bad idea . . .'

'But, Aish, you can't have been there then!' said Utterly. 'Not when the stones were raised up. It was hundreds and thousands of years ago, and you are no older than my uncle! You weren't born then . . .'

'I don't remember when I was born,' said Aish. 'I remember singing my songs in the woods when the great-grandfathers of the oaks were small. It was they who gave me my name. They whisper it among themselves when the wind blows at sundown off the western deeps. Listen, they are whispering it now. Do you hear them? *Aishhh, Aishhh . . .*'

Utterly laughed, because it was simplest to assume that she was teasing. But it was not funny to think of the poor trolls of old being drowned and trampled over. She shivered. 'Aish,' she asked. 'What does the Gorm *want*?'

'I don't know as she *wants* anything exactly,' said Aish. 'The Gorm is the sea and the sea is the Gorm. She is the Power that dwells in the western deeps. She has her

124

rages and her times of gentleness. Many times she has come to trouble Wildsea and scour away the things that folk have built here. That time John Dark met her and drove her back into the sea was just the latest. She has been slumbering since then. But it seems to me she is waking now.'

'Why?' asked Utterly. 'What has woken her?'

'I do not know. But she takes an interest in you, Utterly Dark. And I can see why too. For you are like the places that the ebb tide bares; you do not properly belong to the land or the sea. I saw it that first time we met. It is unusual, for the war between the sea and land is the oldest war in the world, and most things are on one side or the other. Perhaps the Gorm wonders if you are part of our world or hers.'

'I dreamed of a lady standing in the sea. I found her footprints next day on the sand. I . . . I drew an arrow to show her where I lived. But the Man o' Weed came instead.'

'The tideline is the boundary of her realm,' said Aish. 'If she set her pretty white foot on dry land when she is in human form, she would crumble into dust and ashes. I expect that is why she sent a weedling to go peeking in your window, rather than her own self. I think it was just because of her curiosity, not meaning any harm. But be careful. She is still the Gorm. Even her curiosity can be perilous.'

The sun had set, and the clouds above the sea were edged with rose and gold. In the twilight, the voices of the trees came creeping up the slopes of the tor, whispering, 'Aish! Aish!' Then, mingled with the sound of the branches, Utterly heard another voice.

'Utterly!' it shouted.

19

THE RUNAWAY

Mrs Skraeveling had been fretting about Utterly since tea time, when she failed to return to Sundown Watch.

Will had ignored her at first. 'I thought she had gone to the vicarage?' he said. 'She is safe enough with the Dearloves. She will have stayed to supper, I expect, and will come home in the morning.' Eventually he agreed to walk down to Marazea and make sure the girl was all right. When he found that she was not at the vicarage – that the Dearloves had not seen her that day – he too began to grow worried. He borrowed Reverend Dearlove's horse and rode into Marazea. There he met a man who had come down that afternoon from Trollbridge, who said he'd seen the girl cross the river there and go into the Dizzard woods.

So she has gone to see the trolls, thought Will. Any anger he felt for the trouble Utterly was causing vanished away. All he could think of was how scared she had been after her nightmare, and how scared she might be now, up in the woods with those odd, backward people, and night coming on. He had been scared himself most of the time at her age, and it saddened him to think of Utterly's childhood being overshadowed by the same terrors. So he sent a boy running to Sundown Watch to reassure the Skraevelings, then rode on northward, telling himself all the way that he would see Utterly coming towards him around the next bend, or over the next ridge.

But he did not. When he reached Trollbridge without having met her there was nothing for it but to leave the horse at the inn and head into the woods himself. 'Utterly!' he shouted, as the trees closed over him. 'Utterly!'

❖

Aish took Utterly's hand as they went back down from the tor. The trolls had come out of their cottages to see what was happening. Uncle Will climbed up through the gap in the tumbled boundary wall, looked around at them all, and was about to shout, 'Utterly!' again when he saw her.

'I'm here, Uncle Will,' she said, and went to meet him

with her head bowed to show that she was truly sorry for having run away.

'Utterly!' he said, looking so relieved that Utterly thought for a moment he might hug her. Then, as often happens with grown-ups, the relief tipped over into anger. 'Where have you been? Why did you not tell us where you were going? I have missed my Watch, looking for you . . .'

'It is not the girl's fault,' said Aish. 'And we kept our own Watch from my lookout here, and the Gorm's lands did not show themselves tonight. Utterly can write that in your book when she gets home.' She put a friendly arm around Utterly's shoulders. 'She came here to ask my advice, and I thought it best she stay the night, instead of walking home all lonesome in the midnight dark. You can stay here too, if you like.'

'I – ah – well, that is good of you,' said Will. 'But it will not be necessary.' He had recognized Aish as the young woman who had carried him off the beach after the ship-wreck, and felt too embarrassed to meet her eye. Looking down instead at her broad, bare feet, he said, 'I have a horse waiting at Trollbridge. I will ride home with Utterly tonight. Fetch your things, Utterly.'

Utterly ran to fetch her knapsack, which she found stuffed with plump, russet apples. Her new friends called goodbye to her as she hurried back to where Uncle Will was waiting. He has ridden all this way to find me, she thought. She felt embarrassed at putting him to so much trouble, but also quite proud that he had cared enough about her to come looking.

'I'll come with you as far as the bridge,' Aish said. 'I do not know how you will otherwise find your way down all our twisty paths in this owl-light. I do not know how you found your way up them, to be honest.'

❖

They started down through the trees. Will had brought a lantern with him from the Trollbridge inn, and he insisted on going ahead with it to light the way. Aish strode along beside him, telling him he would see more without it if he would only put it out and let his eyes come accustomed to the dark. Utterly followed a little way behind, and she had not gone far when she heard a soft footfall beside her and realized that Egg was there too.

He caught her eye and winked. 'I want to hear what they are saying,' he whispered. 'Listen to them bickering. They are showing off for each other just like them old sea dragons.'

Utterly did not know what he meant, nor what the wink implied. But in the silence of the woods it was impossible not to overhear what Aish and Uncle Will were saying.

'So what advice did you give Utterly?'

'Only to listen to the sea if it talks to her.'

'The sea does not talk.'

'Is that what the learned gentlemen say in England? They live too far from the western deeps, I reckon. They have forgotten the old Gorm.'

'They do not believe in the Gorm. Nor do I. It is nothing but an old wives' tale.'

'Aha, but what if the Gorm believes in *you*? Old wives are reckoned to know a thing or two, on Wildsea.'

'No doubt. But in this age of Reason, modern science has quite exploded such irrational beliefs. Why, in England the sea is viewed as a highway for commerce, and a place for healthful recreations. At Brighton they have bathing machines, like stripy little rooms on wheels, in which people may change in privacy before the attendants roll them down the beach into the waves . . .'

'To drown them?' cried Aish. 'Oh! How horrible! What have they done to deserve such awful ends?'

'Do not distress yourself, Miss Aish. It is not a punishment – people choose to enter the machines, so they may enjoy the benefits of sea-bathing.'

Aish made a soft snorting sound that was half laughter and half contempt. 'Then they must be very great fools in England,' she said, 'and you are a greater one, Will Dark, if you cannot see it.'

On the path behind her, Egg nudged Utterly, and whispered, 'She likes him. They will be married by next summer, I expect.'

131

'Don't be silly,' said Utterly. She was about to add that nobody could possibly want to marry Uncle Will, but the path turned steeply downhill just then, and at the bend the grown-ups stopped.

'Look there,' said Aish, as Egg and Utterly caught up with them. 'You can see the lights of Trollbridge through the trees. Stay on this path another hundred yards and it will bring you to the bridge.' She reached up, took one of the talismans from around her neck and handed it to Utterly. 'Here. This will help keep you safe.'

Will held up his lantern so Utterly could see the thing Aish had placed in her hand. It was a grey-green stone, the size of a quail's egg, with a hole in it, and a much-knotted piece of hairy string threaded through the hole to turn it into a pendant. Faint lines had been etched into the stone, but if they were words Utterly could not read them, and if they were pictures she could not tell what they were of.

'It is only an old stone, but it comes from a place on the heights of this land where the sea has no power at all. It may give the Gorm's weedy-men something to think on if they come troubling you again.'

'Thank you,' said Utterly, slipping the string over her head.

Will said stiffly, 'You are very kind, Miss Aish, but there is really no need . . .'

'It's all right,' said Aish. 'I have plenty more.' She

touched the clutter of talismans on her chest and turned to Utterly. 'I was right about your uncle. He *is* a fool. So till he comes to see sense, you must keep your watch, and I'll keep mine.'

'I will,' Utterly promised. Aish hugged her goodbye. Utterly looked round for Egg, but he seemed to have vanished into the shadows. As she went on down the path with her uncle, Aish called after her, 'I will send the Egg to look in on you in a day or so. If you need me, he can bring word.'

'The Egg is a boy,' Utterly told Uncle Will. 'He is not an actual egg.'

'I am relieved to hear it,' said Will.

❖

Aish stood watching till the small light of their lantern crossed the bridge and vanished among the brighter lights of the inn. Egg dropped out of a tree and landed beside her, visible mostly as a cheeky white grin in the darkness. 'So he's to be your new man, is he, Aish? What you find in the sea is yours for keeps, i'nt it?'

Aish threw a stone at him and he caught it from the air and ran back up the hill ahead of her, laughing.

20

MAGIC OR MADNESS?

The moon had sunk down into the sea long before the tired horse brought Utterly and her uncle home to Sundown Watch. The Skraevelings had waited up for them. Mr Skraeveling fussed over the horse, and Mrs Skraeveling fussed over Utterly. Utterly had slept through most of the ride, wedged in front of Uncle Will in the saddle. She woke up just enough to drink some cocoa and tell Mrs Skraeveling that the trolls did not live in holes in the ground at all, but she was yawning so much she could scarcely get the words out, and after a while Mrs Skraeveling said, 'Tell me all about it in the morning, kitten,' and packed her off to bed.

No one fussed over Will, but Will did not want them to. He sat in the dining room, alone with his thoughts and a dish of toasted cheese. These past two nights had given him much to think about.

The woman Aish had come as a surprise to him. He had thought her just a dull-witted hedge-witch, but talking with her had made him understand she was clever enough to hold her own in conversation with most of the men he knew in London, and engaging enough to outshine most of the ladies, if you overlooked her curious appearance. It was a tragedy that her lively mind had been filled with so many worthless old superstitions and folk beliefs.

That made him think of another lively mind: Utterly's, which he feared was being stuffed with more of the same nonsense. Indeed, how could it be otherwise, when the girl's only sources of knowledge were Aish, and the Skraevelings, and crazy old Thurza Froy? Drewe had tried to give her an education, but even Drewe had believed in sea magic by the end, it seemed.

When the Skraevelings had gone to bed, he fetched a hammer and a chisel from the tool shed and climbed the stairs to Drewe's study, where he dragged the locked strongbox down from the top shelf. It was time for him to know Drewe's final secrets. The lock seemed almost impregnable, but he turned the box round and succeeded in forcing the tip of the chisel under the lid, hammering it in with a few swift blows until the hinges gave way and he was able to lift the lid off.

He did not know what he had been expecting. Treasure

trove? There was only a little bracelet of faded pink coral and a few sheets of paper, folded. He took those back to his own room. He had already guessed what they were. He recognized them by their size and the weight and weave of the paper. Sure enough, when he had lit the oil lamp, he saw they were pages which Drewe had carefully cut out of the Log.

They were entries from twelve years before, the summer after Will's departure for England.

7th May. The Islands are very clear tonight. This afternoon I saw her again, her head breaking the surface ten feet offshore. She pushed her black hair back from her face and held my gaze for a long time.

8th May. I walked on the beaches all day. The Hidden Lands were visible throughout the afternoon, like low clouds on the horizon, but I knew they were no clouds. At sundown they grew very clear, and there was a light upon the shore.

9th May. Today I saw her for the first time clear of the water. She was on the rocks in Blanchmane's Cove, walking very careful, like a cat, as if she is not used to anything solid underfoot and each step was curious to her. She will not come further than the tideline. Her hair would be black, I think, even if it were not always wet. Her skin is fair, with a blueness about her lips and the tips of her fingers and toes. She saw me and dived back into the sea with a splash. I waited a long while, but she did not resurface.

10th May. Why has she come? Where has she come from? Can she exist under the sea like a fish, or must she surface from time to time to breathe, as the seals do? Perhaps she is a seal. Perhaps I have gone mad and am imagining a lost seal is a mermaiden? Yet not quite a mermaiden, for she has no fish-tail, as the sirens in the storybooks all do. I saw her small footprints in the sand today, a chain of them leading out of the sea and back to the sea, perfect footprints, and perfectly human.

17th May. Thalassa. Tethys. Tiamat. Sedna. T'ien-Fei. The Gorm.

21st May. We met today again, upon the sand in Gull Cove. The cliffs stood sentinel, shining with the rain that blew in off the sea. I tried to make her stay but she broke free and ran to the sea and the sea took her. I scuffed out the marks we had made in the sand lest some other shore-walker should read them.

Then followed two weeks of ordinary observations –

26th May. No sighting tonight, the cloud low.

2nd June. The sky clear to the horizon but no sighting, it is as if the Islands were never there.

And then, scribbled under another routine entry on the 16th of June:

I stood upon the reef at Gull Cove again and called to her, and the waves came and went, and there was no answer. She has returned to the Hidden Lands, and the Hidden Lands have returned to wherever it is that they hide.

I must put all this from my mind.

As he read the strange account, Will could almost hear his brother's voice. What had happened on the sand at Gull Cove? What had made dull, unimaginative Drewe start groping for similes and metaphors like a poet, the sentinel cliffs, her steps like a cat's . . . Who was she? A fantasy? An hallucination? Thalassa, Tethys – those were names of goddesses; goddesses of the sea. But why would Drewe have added the Gorm's name to that list? The Gorm was a monster, not a goddess. Though Will remembered how Aish had spoken of the Gorm as 'her'. Perhaps there was no difference between goddesses and monsters . . .

He flicked that thought away, and turned to the final page. It came from later, the February of the following year. There were a few terse, business-like entries (*The wind from the North and v. chill, the sea empty*).

Then on the 20th:

I saw the Hidden Lands tonight. I am watching them as I sit writing here. The three peaks v. clear, and the lights upon the shore. Are those the windows of the palace she once whispered to me of? I will rise at first light and wait for her upon the beach.

And on the 21st:

This morning in Blanchmane's Cove I found – the next line had been heavily crossed out, then – *I thought at first it was a leather bag washed up, but when I went close I found it out to be a great purse such as the dogfish hatch from, but much larger. Green-black it was, and shining. It moved with a sluggish motion as though something within it struggled to break free. I touched it with the toe of my boot, and a split opened in it, and through that split a tiny hand appeared, a human hand, palest pink, the fingers clenching and unclenching, and as the slime from inside the thing drained out, the infant that lay within it filled her lungs with air and started to howl.*

I set to and pulled her free – a baby girl, much beslimed but quite well to all appearances. Not knowing what else to do, I wrapped the child in my cloak and carried her home. I did not tell Mr and Mrs S about the egg-sac; I gave them to understand that I had found her cast up in a basket or some crude manner of coracle, and that the tide had taken it away again. The Skraevelings think she is the lone survivor of a wreck, and that Rev. Dearlove and his wife will find a home for her. But there have been no wrecks reported, and the child's home is here with me. I know her little kitten-face. She has her mother's eyes. She comes from the Hidden Lands. She is—

And then another crossing-out, so heavy that Will

139

could not see the words which had been erased even when he held the page up to the light.

He read through the entries again, searching between Drewe's words for some meaning he had missed. By the time he finished it was very late, and he was trembling. Poor Drewe's account had been so vivid that it was almost tempting to believe it, but of course such things could not be. There was no magic here, there was only madness.

He put the pages in the drawer of his dressing table and went downstairs to Utterly's room. After the alarms of the previous night it had been agreed that she might keep the door open and a lamp burning. Will had expected her to close the shutters too, and draw the heavy curtains across them, for fear of what might come peeping in at her window, but when he looked into her room he saw that both shutters and curtains were open wide. If anything came prowling, Utterly had wanted to see it.

Brave girl, Will thought, wondering if he would have had such courage at her age. He stood looking down at her, her sleeping face on the pillow, one small hand loosely clenched beside it. Clutched in her fingers was the holed stone Aish had given her. It is up to me to save her, he thought, and suddenly he felt quite desperate to protect her. She was his one firm link with Drewe, and he would not let her grow up in groundless fear, believing that the Gorm was watching her, and weed-men walked the shores of Wildsea, and babies were hatched from mermaids' purses.

He had to prove to her that none of it was true. He had to prove it to the Skraevelings, and Aish, and the Dearloves too. He would find a way to shake everyone on Wildsea from their dreams and make them see the world as it really was: ruled by reason; free from myths and monsters. He, Will Dark, would tear down the legends of the Gorm as you might tear down heavy, dusty drapes to let the daylight in . . .

But how?

Outside the window, the night was starting to fade. The sea rolled and roared and rubbed itself against the shore. The ring of old stones on the headland stood out black against the greyness in the west.

Will stood and stared at them, and suddenly he knew what he must do.

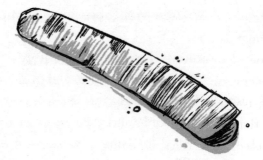

21

MEASURING THE STONES

Utterly slept late on the morning after her adventure to the Dizzard. Even when she was up and dressed she still had the feeling she was dreaming, and her legs were stiff from her long walk the day before. But hot buttered toast woke her properly, and when Lucy and Horatio arrived to reclaim their father's horse she was able to tell them all the details of her adventures. 'Aish is a very important person on the Dizzard,' she explained. 'As important as your father is in Marazea at least; probably more. I talked to her for ages. She argued with my uncle Will, but you could tell they like each other really and he was only showing off.' That had sounded silly when Egg said it, but repeating it made Utterly feel rather wise. 'They shall be married by next summer, I expect.'

'But she is a *troll*!' objected Lucy. 'She will probably eat him!'

'She is a very nice troll,' said Utterly. 'And quite a pretty one, once you get used to her. And she likes eating cakes, not people. I declare, Lucy, she loves cakes even more than you do.'

'*Nobody* loves cakes more than I do,' said Lucy. 'Would Mrs Skraeveling have a cake about at all? It is a long walk from the vicarage and Horatio and I shall need fortifying before we ride the horse home.'

There *was* a cake about: one of the many advantages of living with Mrs Skraeveling was that there was *always* a cake about. When Lucy and Horatio had been fortified and waved off down the cliff track on the patient horse, Utterly went looking for her uncle. 'He was in the study last I seen him, kitten,' Mr Skraeveling told her, but when she looked in the study she found no Uncle Will, only a lot of old volumes of the Log taken down from the shelves and left scattered all anyhow on the writing table and across the carpet.

That surprised Utterly, who had never noticed Uncle Will show much interest in the old Logs before. She hoped he had been reflecting on what Aish had told him, and was taking his job of Watcher more seriously. Then, glancing down from the window, she saw him way out on St Chyan's Head, making measurements with a tape measure among the circle of standing stones.

Utterly had not often walked right out to the stones, and when she ventured out there to join her uncle she remembered why. For one thing, the path that led out to the headland was so narrow, and the drops on either side so steep, and the rocks below so sharp and jagged, that it made her feel dizzy just to walk along it. For another, the stones themselves were weirdly frightening.

Knobbly granite fingers as tall as men, they looked like a ring of hooded figures surrounding a broader, flatter stone called St Chyan's Chair which lay on its side in the grass. As she stepped into the ring, Utterly felt the hairs on her arms and the back of her neck prickle with unease. It was that same sense of being watched that she had felt before, but it was even stronger now. It was as if, somewhere in the west, keen eyes had opened and swung their gaze like the beam of a lighthouse across the sea until they found Utterly standing there among the stones.

Uncle Will did not seem to feel it. He was kneeling beside St Chyan's Chair, using the old stone as a desk while he scribbled numbers in pencil on a scrap of paper. The tape measure clutched between his teeth streamed out in the wind, trying to tie itself in knots. When he looked round and saw Utterly watching him he took the tape out of his mouth and passed it to her. 'Utterly! Good girl. You can lend me a hand. I am endeavouring to calculate the angles between the stones.'

'Why?' asked Utterly.

'In the spirit of scientific enquiry. I don't believe anyone has ever properly recorded this circle before. Wildsea folk say it is not even possible to count the stones, but I have already proven *that* tale to be nonsense: there are nine of them. Recording and measuring and understanding things is how we overcome foolish fears and superstitions, Utterly. Would you hold the end of the tape against the base of that stone, and let me take the other . . . ? Thank you . . . Besides,' he shouted, from the far side of the circle, 'I wish to compare our circle to Dr Stukeley's accounts of the famous Druid temple at Stonehenge. I believe our stones were put here by Druids too, and doubtless for the same purpose.'

Utterly frowned. When he had taken his measurement and noted it down, she said, 'But Uncle Will, everyone knows the Gormstones were put here to mark the place where the fire was lit. The magic fire that called the Gorm out of the Hidden Lands. Then the olden-days people put the stones here as a warning, to tell everyone who came after, "Don't go lighting fires upon St Chyan's Head, for trouble comes of it."'

'Yes, yes,' said Uncle Will. 'That is the *story*. But you do realize, Utterly, it cannot be true? There is no Gorm, and there are no Hidden Lands, or, if there are, they are merely a mirage, a kind of *Fata Morgana* which appears above the sea in certain types of weather. The people

145

who raised these stones had seen them too, perhaps, and wove them into whatever rituals they performed here. No doubt they *did* light fires up here, to mark all those turnings of the year which your friend Miss Aish warned us to beware of. I suspect the entire legend of the Gorm is really nothing more than a frayed folk-memory of those ancient Druidic ceremonies . . .'

He sounded so happy as he said it, and so certain he was right, that for a moment Utterly wanted to believe him. How reassuring it would be to think that the Hidden Lands were only a trick of the weather, and the old Gorm nothing but a story. But even though she had turned her back to the sea she could still feel that cold gaze fixed firmly on her, like something scratching softly at her shoulder blades. As if some great, cold mind out there in the ocean was considering what these two tiny humans might be doing, creeping about like ants upon the clifftop.

Uncle Will glanced nervously at the horizon and said, 'They knew their business, those old Druids. This place *does* have an eerie atmosphere. It is easy to see how people could come to believe that . . .' His words trailed off into silence.

Utterly wondered what he was seeing, out there where the edge of the sea blended into the hem of the sky. She was too nervous to turn round and look.

Uncle Will shook himself like a dog, and laughed. 'But

it is the job of educated people to explode such notions,' he said. 'I intend to free Wildsea from its sea terrors, once and for all.'

22

THE BOAT

The sea brewed up a fog that night. At daybreak it still lay thickly over the coast. Sundown Watch and its gardens and the headland with its ring of stones stood up out of the vapours like a little island of their own. 'That old Gorm has been stirring up its cauldron,' said Mrs Skraeveling over breakfast.

Will surprised everyone by rising early and eating with the rest of them. When he was finished he rose and put on his three-cornered hat. 'I am off beachcombing,' he said. 'Utterly, I have left some lessons for you in the study. I fear I have been neglecting your education.'

He left the house and set off down the cliff track, the fog very thick all around him, the sound of the invisible sea surprisingly clear as it rumbled and hissed against the feet of the cliffs. He passed through Marazea and found his way onto the Undercliff, where he had not been since he was a boy. He and some of the village lads used to dare each other to go and knock upon the sea-witch's door, but they had never even managed to come in sight of her shack before their courage deserted them and they fled back to safer ground. Today he kept going, pushing his way through the dripping bushes and mist-bespangled spider webs until wood smoke mingled with the fog and Thurza Froy's hovel appeared ahead.

There was no sign of life, and no answer when Will knocked on the door. He circled the shack, kicked idly at the blackened remains of a bonfire, and called, 'Mrs Froy!' to no avail. Then he became aware of a repetitive sound somewhere below him. He found a path which twisted steeply down through wet heather and onto shingle at the top of a small beach. There, upturned on a set of trestles, was the only boat he had ever seen on the western coasts of Wildsea. It was a trim little boat, built from planks of blond and silver wood. Thurza Froy was leaning over it, scraping its keel smooth with a plane.

'Watcher,' she said, when she saw him standing there. She did not stop her work. 'I heard you'd drowned.'

'And I heard witches went to sea in eggshells,' said Will. 'Yet here you are, building a fine boat.'

Thurza nodded, accepting his praise. 'I shall need her soon,' she said. 'Can't you see the Gorm's breath all around you? The Hidden Lands are revealing themselves. This boat will carry me there, so I can find my Davey again, and we shall gather up all the treasures that are ours by rights.'

Will thought how pathetic it was that the old crone still imagined her husband was alive. He wondered how many years it taken her to build the boat out of scraps of driftwood and the nails she traded for curses and love potions. But he said, 'I remember my father telling me the story of your first expedition. The diving suit you made. Remarkable. You were a woman ahead of your time, Mrs Froy. A woman of science.'

'I seen 'em,' said Thurza. She kept working the plane. Wood shavings gathered about her feet like shorn blond curls. 'Down below the waves they was, and not so far down neither. The Hidden Lands.'

'They lie beneath the sea?'

'Beneath it, or upon it, or above it, it is all the same to them. They ain't part of this world. They are their own place, and they appear wherever the Gorm pleases. But on the day me and Davey saw them, they lay ten fathoms deep.'

'Will you tell me of them?' asked Will.

'Don't like to talk of it,' the old woman muttered.

'A pity.' Will reached in his coat pocket and took out a flask of whisky. He did not like whisky, but he had found a half-bottle in the liquor cabinet at Sundown Watch, and brought some with him, thinking it might prove useful.

He held the flask out to Thurza Froy and said, 'That must be thirsty work.'

She looked at him, set down her plane and came to snatch the flask, gulping down its contents greedily.

'We were speaking of the Hidden Lands,' he said.

Thurza wiped her hand across her lips and belched. 'I'll tell 'ee,' she said, 'but you'll not believe me.'

'I might,' said Will, and sat down on an old lobster pot to listen.

'Thirty mile west o' St Chyan's Head we seen 'em,' said the sea-witch. 'The sea was calm that day. Unnatural calm, some might say. Smooth as a window-glass it was, and when my Davey an' me looked down into it we saw the Hidden Lands as clear as if we was peepin' through a window. Towers and gardens down there underneath the waves we saw. Statues with golden crowns. A palace with golden roofs. The glow of all that gold shone up through the waves and lit our faces yellow like we was holding buttercups under our chins.

'My Davey dropped anchor. "Wish me luck, Thurza girl!" he said. Then we sealed him in his diving suit and over the side he went, with me paying out a cable so he did not sink too fast. When he touched bottom he jerked it thrice to say all's well, and I started pumping air down to him with the fireplace bellows. But between pumpings I kept sneaking looks over the side, down at where my Davey was. He was turning round an' round in wonderment down there till I feared he'd tie his air-tube in a knot. I wished he would stop gawping an' start gathering up our treasures. And that was when I saw *her*.'

'Saw who?' asked Will.

'*Her*. She come out of one of them dark doorways. Dressed all in white she was, with her long black hair a-streaming and a-swirling like weeds in a tide-pool. *She* didn't need no diving suit. She went strolling towards my Davey as bold as brass. He had his back to her and hadn't seen her.

'Well, I wasn't having him a-dallying with no mermaid in the deep. I started hauling in the cable that we'd tied around his middle. But no Davey come up with it. Some clever fingers down there in the deeps had undone my knots, and all I got back was the cable itself. Then I reeled in the breathing-tube, thinking that might drag him up, but it had been sliced through.'

'So he was drowned?'

'Ain't you been listening, Watcher? It was *her*, that lady down below, that had done them things. She'd took a fancy to my Davey-boy, and kept him for herself. *She* didn't need no diving suit, and now nor did he. Water is as good as air to them as dwell under the Gorm's enchantments.'

'You saw him down there?' asked Will. 'Alive?'

'I didn't see nothing after that,' muttered Thurza, taking another swig from Will's flask and looking disgusted to find it empty. 'And why not? Because the

Gorm came for me, that's why not. I looked down hoping to see Davey, and there was the Gorm's great hand rising up out of the deep. It grasped the boat and crushed and splintered it and left me clinging to a spar. I washed up next day on Wildsea nine-tenths drownded. And here I been ever since, watching the sea, learning its mysteries, looking for ways to get back to them Hidden Lands and fetch my Davey home.'

'A most fascinating account,' said Will, although it was clear to him that most of the yarn had been nonsense. The submerged ruins were intriguing, but the so-called Gorm had probably been nothing but a freak squall. As for the mermaid, Will guessed she was a story the old woman had invented to spare herself the blame for sending her husband to his death in that shoddy diving suit. The only thing that troubled Will was the mention of her long black hair – so unlike the mermaids in stories, but so like the person Drewe claimed to have met upon the shore. Could they be the same woman? For a moment he felt as if the screens of science and logic he had erected around himself were being pulled aside to reveal an older and a stranger world, where wild magic whispered in the waves.

He reminded himself to get a grip. As the only man of science upon the island, it was his duty to keep a level head. The black-haired mermaid was coincidence, no more. Or maybe Drewe had found his way to the

Undercliff before him, and coaxed Thurza's tale out of her, and woven parts of it into his own deranged fancies.

'Fascinating,' he said again, and pointed to the upturned boat. 'So that is what your boat is for? You mean to make another attempt to reach these Hidden Lands?'

'Aye,' said Thurza. 'But not while the Gorm waits there, guarding it. First the Gorm must rise. When the Gorm walks, the Hidden Lands stay in our world for a while.'

'And you think the Gorm will come soon?'

Thurza shrugged. 'It is awake. It is watching. Don't you feel its eyes on you? But it needs the call. It needs summoning. A fire would do it.'

'But you light fires almost nightly, and no Gorm appears.'

'I tries my best. But it needs to be the right fire, and in the right place. And you Darks have barred me from Gorm's Head.'

'Well, I am sorry for your inconvenience,' said Will. 'Perhaps I can make it up to you? You see, I hope to engage you as my assistant in a small experiment . . .'

23

THE EXPERIMENT

No one had given much thought to Utterly's education since Mr Dark drowned, and Utterly had been hoping they would carry on that way, for she had not missed the twelve times table or her Latin verbs one bit. But when she went up to the study that morning, she found the task that Uncle Will had set her was only to copy out a map of the Autumn Isles, and she did not mind that at all.

She enjoyed drawing maps. It was satisfying, carefully putting in all the wriggly bits around each island's edge, and writing their names on them in red ink. She drew dotted lines to show the major shipping routes, and a red cross on the north end of the Dizzard to mark the place where Uncle Will's ship was wrecked.

In early afternoon, when patches of sea and hill were showing through the fog as if they were thinking about becoming permanent, the boy called Egg came stomping up the track to Sundown Watch. Utterly left off her map-making and hurried to the kitchens to watch him gulp down a cup of milk which Mrs Skraeveling had given him. He wore a shirt and coat today as well as his breeches. There was a hat like a shapeless felt bag on his head, and drops of sweat beading his forehead and his nose. Utterly liked the smell of him; damp earth and cows.

'What are you looking at?' he asked, setting down the empty cup. The milk had given him a white moustache.

'A cat may look at a king,' said Utterly. 'Why have you come?'

'For Aish, o' course. She wanted me to check you come home safe after the other night.'

'Quite safe, thank you,' said Utterly, wondering if she should write a note for him to take back to the Dizzard: *Dear Miss Aish, thank you for a delightful evening . . .* It would be good manners, but Utterly was not sure Aish would care much about good manners. Come to that, could Aish even read?

'Can Aish read and write?' she asked Egg.

'Course she can!' said Egg disgustedly. 'She went to the school in Stack and learned her letters. The kids there called her troll-girl, but she picked them up and threw them in a ditch, and there was no more trouble from them after that. She wrote this for me to give you.'

He reached inside his grubby coat and drew out a roll of papery birch-bark. Utterly unrolled it, and saw that Aish's handwriting was almost as neat as her own. *Dear Utterly*, the birch-bark letter read. *Remember that you may come and see me any time you wish. Please tell your foolish uncle Will the same. He will need my help, should the old Gorm rise. Your friend, A*

'It is your uncle she really wants to see,' said Egg wisely. 'And you know what that means.'

'Oh yes,' said Utterly, although she didn't quite. She could not think of anything else to say on that subject, so she added, 'Uncle Will is beachcombing.'

'On the beach?' asked Egg.

'That's where it's usually done.'

'Dangerous,' said the boy, shaking his head. 'Have you checked on him?'

Utterly was suddenly ashamed that she had not. Of course it was not safe to let Uncle Will wander around on beaches on his own, not when he was too silly to believe in the dangers. 'Mrs Skraeveling!' she called. 'Where did Uncle Will go?'

'He was off down on that old Undercliff this morning,' said the housekeeper, poking her head out of the pantry. 'But Skraeveling says he came home around noon, and now he's gone down into Blanchmane's Cove, where we must pray he don't end up a-drowning himself.'

❖

The fog had almost gone and golden autumn sunlight was spreading itself like butter over the clifftops. In Blanchmane's Cove the tide was low. Uncle Will was walking along the shingle at the top of the beach carrying a big baulk of driftwood. Egg dropped on his belly at the cliff's edge to spy on him, and Utterly threw herself down beside him. They watched as Uncle Will tossed the driftwood onto a big heap that he had gathered at the foot of the cliff path.

'What is he doing that for?' wondered Egg.

A chough, disturbed by his voice, took off from a ledge a few feet below and slid away on the wind, calling out angrily. Utterly hoped her uncle would not notice, but of course Uncle Will had been raised on these shores, and he recognized a chough's alarm call. He looked up and saw the two faces peering down at him.

He waved. 'Utterly! And, ah, Egg . . . Come down here and make yourselves useful!'

They scrambled down the steep path, and Uncle Will stepped back to dodge the little landslips of loose stones they dislodged as they went. The heap of driftwood he had assembled was taller than Utterly. 'You can help me get all this up the cliff,' he said.

'What for?' asked Egg, who had seen Mr Skraeveling's impressive log-pile in the shed outside the kitchen and knew Sundown Watch did not need extra firewood.

'I have decided to make an experiment,' said Uncle Will.

❖

'It is going to be a big one,' said Egg, when he and Utterly had spent twenty minutes or so ferrying armloads of driftwood up the cliff and adding them to the heap Uncle Will was assembling at the top.

'What is going to be a big one?' asked Utterly.

'This experiment he is making,' said Egg, starting down again, and Utterly realized that he thought an experiment must be a fancy piece of furniture, like an escritoire or an ottoman.

But even she did not understand what Uncle Will was actually planning; not until the wood was all brought up, and he pointed out to the headland where the Gormstones stood and said, 'That is where we are taking it next.'

'But what for?' asked Utterly, although she could already guess the answer. That plummeting sensation in her innards told her what he was planning before he could speak the word.

'A bonfire,' said Will.

'Not on St Chyan's Head!' declared Utterly, amazed that even her uncle would be foolish enough to contemplate such a thing. 'Not at the Gormstones! You mustn't! You can't!'

'Indeed I must!' laughed Will. 'And I can!'

'Oh, sir, you must not light any fires upon St Chyan's Head,' she explained carefully, as if he were a child too stupid to understand the dangers – for what other explanation could there be but stupidity? 'It is a magic place, and no one must ever light a fire there, because it will summon up the Gorm.'

Will stooped to look into her face. He had pulled off his coat and waistcoat and his loose linen shirt was covered in sand and soft splinters from the driftwood. 'You know I do not believe in this old Gorm, Utterly,' he said. 'I think it is nothing but a legend. So I am going to light a fire here at the Gormstones, just as in the stories, and we shall see what happens. The weather is clear, and we are high enough that everyone from Gull Point to the Dizzard will see our blaze. When the Gorm does not come, they will have to stop believing in it. It is so simple I am amazed no one has tried it before.'

'But what if . . .' said Utterly, who thought she understood perfectly why no one had tried it before, '. . . what if the Gorm *does* come?'

Will looked at her sadly, as if he had expected better of her. 'Well, Utterly, my ancestor's famous sword still hangs

160

on the dining-room wall. If the monster does appear, I shall simply have to cut off its head and render Wildsea safely Gormless again.'

But he didn't really mean that, Utterly knew. How could he be prepared to battle the Gorm if he didn't believe in it to begin with? Her face felt hot. His stupidity, his treachery, made her want to cry.

'Now, help me get all this firewood out to the stones,' said Uncle Will. He gathered up a big load himself and set off along the narrow way to the headland. Utterly watched him go. Then she turned and looked at Egg, and they both fled, through the gate and back up the garden towards the house.

'I'll tell Mr Skraeveling,' Utterly said as they ran. 'He won't let Uncle Will do it.'

'And what if he can't stop him?' asked Egg. 'We need to tell Aish. Aish will know what to do.'

Utterly knew he was right. If only Aish were here, she would put a stop to Uncle Will's folly. But Aish was still on the Dizzard, and Utterly knew from experience how far from Sundown Watch that was; she still had blisters from the walk. 'It will take ages for you to reach her . . .' she said.

'The tide's not turned yet,' said Egg. 'I'll run along the beaches to Trollbrook Mouth. It's flat that way, instead of up and down all them old cliffs.'

'Good luck,' Utterly said, and watched him go haring

across the walled garden to the gate and away down the track to Marazea at a steady trot. Much of the afternoon had worn away while they were dragging driftwood up the cliff for Uncle Will. The sun was westering, the shadows stretching themselves out like sleepy cats. The wind had dropped, and the sea was very quiet. Everything seemed to be holding its breath.

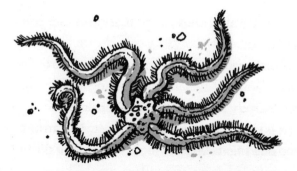

24

THE DRIFTWOOD FIRE

M r Skraeveling was clearing out the gutterings on the landward side of the house. Utterly stood at the foot of his ladder and called up to him as if he were God. 'Uncle Will is making a bonfire at the Gormstones and you mustn't let him!'

A splat of wet black leaves came down, and one of Mr Skraeveling's rare, surprising curses. 'He's doing *what* now?'

Utterly held the ladder while the old man came down it, then they set out together around the house and along the path to the stones. Uncle Will was shaping his driftwood into a clumsy pyramid. Utterly consoled herself with the thought that he might not know how to light a fire, but it still chilled her to see him building one,

163

there in the very spot where that other fire had burned so long ago.

'Begging your pardon, but this is no place to light a fire, Master Will, sir,' said Mr Skraeveling. Utterly thought he sounded very polite, all things considered.

'It is the very place, Skraeveling,' said Uncle Will. 'I'm astonished no one has done it before. You'd think some roistering lad from the village would have climbed in over the wall. Or one of my more philosophically-minded forebears might have tried it. I know old Thurza Froy keeps lighting her little fires down on the Undercliff, but that's the wrong place, isn't it? She admitted as much herself, when I paid a call on her this morning. It is a fire on St Chyan's Head that will call the Gorm, that's what we Wildsea folk have been taught down all these years. So, let us experiment! This is a new age, Mr Skraeveling, an enlightened age. We don't have to believe in old tales any more. Not when we can test them against the evidence of our own eyes.'

Mr Skraeveling took off his hat and scratched the top of his head. He was an intelligent man but not an educated one, and all those long words Master Will had used – 'philosophical', 'experiment', 'enlightened' – well, who was Jan Skraeveling to judge if an idea was wise or not when it came wrapped up in words like those? He screwed up his face and said, 'I still don't like it, sir.'

Will, walking past to fetch more fuel for his growing

164

fire, paused and laid a hand on Mr Skraeveling's shoulder. 'I am not asking you to like it, Skraeveling. It is frightening, I know. We are breaking a taboo. But tomorrow, when you wake up knowing that there is no Gorm and no Hidden Lands . . . You will find you like it well enough tomorrow.'

He strode away. Mr Skraeveling looked helplessly at Utterly. 'What can I do, kitten? He is the Watcher, and I am not.'

You can stop him! Utterly wanted to shout. *Hit him! Tie him up! Lock him in the linen cupboard! Fetch your pistol and point it at him and tell him you'll blow his silly brains out if he sets a light to that bonfire he is building!* But she knew Mr Skraeveling would do none of those things, and she knew she wouldn't either, even if she had been big enough to knock Uncle Will down.

Because, what if he was right? His long words were working their spell on her too. Uncle Will knew so much more about the world than she did.

When he came past again with his next armload of wood she said, 'Uncle Will, do you really think the Hidden Lands are just a . . . that thing you called them earlier, a *Farting Gardener* . . .'

'A *Fata Morgana*,' said Uncle Will, laughing. 'It is a type of mirage.'

Utterly tried hard to be reassured. She so wanted to believe him, and so did Mr Skraeveling, she could tell.

165

They went back together into the house, leaving Uncle Will to finish his preparations on the headland. 'He is like a man possessed,' muttered Mrs Skraeveling when her husband told her what was happening.

No one spoke much during dinner. Utterly kept glancing at the clock, thinking of Egg running along the beaches and wondering if he had reached the Dizzard yet. Uncle Will came to the table late, with his shirt all stained with tar from some ships' timbers he had added to his fire. Utterly wondered if the timbers might have washed ashore from the wreck of the *Boldventure*, like him. She was just getting ready to ask him when she heard the distant clanging of the bell at the front gate.

Will stood up, leaving his treacle pudding half-finished. Utterly was generally in favour of people leaving their puddings unfinished, because it meant that she could finish them herself, but this seemed ominous.

'That will be our visitor,' said Will.

'Whoever it is, they are ringing the old bell off its bracket by the sound of it,' grumbled Mr Skraeveling, but Will was already out of earshot, pulling his boots on in the hallway. Utterly and the others left the table and followed him as he strode out of the house and across the garden to unbolt the gate.

'Mrs Froy,' he said, stepping aside to let the sea-witch in. 'I am delighted you could join us.'

Thurza Froy slunk into the garden, bringing with her a

166

noxious smell, which probably had something to do with the large and none-too-fresh crab dangling on a string around her neck. She eyed Utterly and the Skraevelings with about as much affection as she had shown Mrs Dearlove that day on the Undercliff. She bared her long yellow teeth at them and hissed.

'Master Will!' said Mrs Skraeveling. 'Whatever are you thinking, bringing this old baggage here? The wall was built for the purpose of stopping such folk getting out onto our headland, and here you are letting her through the gate like she's the Queen of Sheba!'

'Calm yourself, Mrs Skraeveling,' said Will, closing the gate. 'It will convince nobody if I light the Gorm-fire myself. When no Gorm appears they will only say I lacked sufficient faith, or did not know the proper magic words to chant. But no one could accuse Mrs Froy of not knowing her business.'

'And if any do, I shall call upon the Gorm to squelch them with its vasty feet and skewer them with its mighty talons!' cackled Thurza Froy.

'Precisely,' said Will, wrinkling his nose at the stink of her as she scuttled past him and vanished around the side of the house.

The sea-witch knew where she was going, and she went there at a run, before Will could change his mind. She had dreamed for years of this, but even in her dreams she had never imagined one of the fine gentlemen at

167

Sundown Watch would ever be fool enough to let her just walk in through the gate. She had never expected the Watcher of Wildsea himself would drag up driftwood from the shore for her fire. She gave a cackle of delight when she saw it, and went quickly out onto the head-land with Uncle Will following her and Utterly and the Skraevelings following him.

Thurza walked once around the fire, then started to tug timber out of it. 'This won't do,' she muttered. 'Nor that . . .' She tossed a hunk of ship's planking aside, then a sea-bleached branch.

'What is wrong with them?' asked Will indignantly.

'Wood from the Hidden Lands, that's what we need,' said Thurza, intent on her work. She pulled a big old silver-white tree root from the pile, sniffed it, stuck out her tongue and licked it. 'This will do. And that . . .'

Will looked out across the sea. The sun was a hand's-breadth off the horizon. Normally he would be climbing the Tower around now. 'Enough,' he told the sea-witch. 'It will all burn, wherever it has floated from. It is time we lit it, while there is still light enough to see the Hidden Lands by, if they are there.'

'They are there,' said Thurza sulkily. 'I seen 'em. Like buttercups it was, the light from all them golden roofs, all lovely yellow . . .' She stood swaying for a moment, relishing the memory, then sniffed loudly and snatched the tinderbox Will was holding out to her. Utterly and the Skraevelings watched from outside the circle of stones as the sea-witch crouched over the fire and struck sparks onto the dry grass and oily rags which Will had stuffed between the timbers as kindling.

After a moment a trickle of pale blue smoke emerged and climbed straight up into the still air. Thurza edged back and watched in silence till the first flames showed. They were very pale, as if they had been torn out of white paper, and they made papery little noises as they poked their heads up through the gaps between the driftwood. She gave a grunt of satisfaction and turned towards the west.

Spreading her arms out wide, she shouted in a high, unnatural voice:

'Sea, rise! Waves, roll!

Let drowned men walk and drowned bells toll!

Great Gorm come, eat up the land!

Let fishes swim where now I stand!'

The words echoed from the Gormstones and rang out into the strangely quiet, strangely still air. Mrs Skraeveling touched her husband's arm and said quietly, 'This ain't right, Skraeveling. This ain't Christian. I reckon poor Master Will has gone sea-mad, to allow such a performance. You take yourself down to Marazea and fetch Reverend Dearlove.'

'Good thinking, Carrie,' said her husband. 'The parson will talk some sense into Master Will.'

'And tell him he might need a whole bucket of holy water to put out that witch-fire!' his wife called after him, as he hurried away. She took Utterly's hand. 'Now then, kitten, let us go back into the house and clear the dishes, and leave this nasty old article to her chantings and her conflaggerations . . .'

But Utterly could not leave the headland. She did not want the Gorm-fire to be happening, but now that it was, she felt she had to stay and see what came of it. So far, it seemed to be achieving nothing at all, except to make Uncle Will look smug. The sea-witch stood there with her arms stretched out as far as they would go and spoke her spell now loud, now low, until the words lost all meaning and became just a sound, like the gentle lapping of the waves on the rocks below. Nothing answered her call.

Then Utterly realized that the sea, which had been so quiet until a moment ago, had begun to break loudly against the base of the cliffs, and the smoke, which had been rising up so straight from the driftwood fire, was bending inland on a wind from the west.

25

FROM THE GREAT DEEPS

Egg liked running. He was good at it too. Quick, steady, and sure-footed. In Marazea Bay the low-tide sand stretched out flat and smooth and still damp from the sea, like a wide road of brown sugar leading north. Egg went pounding along it, dunes to his right, surf to his left, scrambling over the walls of the old town of Marazea which the Gorm had so trampled on its previous visit that they were little more than lumps under the sand. He ran as fast as an arrow and as straight, except where there was a tide-pool or a mound of cast-up weed. Those he went around. They belonged to the sea, and were best avoided.

He was at Crannock Mouth by the time the last ember of the sinking sun was finally snuffed out by the clouds. He waded the river there and ran on, but the mood of the shore had changed. The waves were louder, and seemed suddenly hungry as they rushed in across the sand. When one almost touched his feet Egg decided it was time to leave the beach, and scrambled up the cliffs where the old turf fort stood. There he paused, looking back, heart thumping, breathless, proud of himself for running so far and so fast.

Below him on the sand all the heaps of weed which the last tide had abandoned there were being collared by the waves, as if the sea had remembered it had a use for them after all. Egg had a nasty feeling that some of the heaps were not waiting for the waves to reach them but just making their own way down the beach into the surf, creeping over the sand like shaggy black legless hounds answering the huntsman's call. But it was hard to be certain in that dying light. The only thing he could see clearly was the pale fire that flickered upon St Chyan's Head.

Egg gave a quick shiver at the wrongness of it all. He hoped Utterly Dark was safe. She was all right, was Utterly Dark, and he had decided to make it his business to keep her from harm. So he must not wait here too long and let his tired legs get stiff; they still had a way to carry him yet.

He ran on across the ramparts and ditches of the fort and down towards the Trollbrook. He knew of a place a half-mile upstream where he could cross the river by jumping from boulder to boulder. Long before he reached it, he was already yelling for Aish. Aish would know what to do.

172

The fire crackled. The sea-witch continued her mindless chant. The rising breeze ruffled Uncle Will's hair as he turned to smile at Utterly. 'You see?' he said. 'No islands. No monster. Nothing.'

Thurza Froy stopped chanting, lowered her arms and spat into the grass. 'The Gorm hears me,' she said. 'It sees me. But it ain't ready to show itself.'

'How unfortunate,' said Will. 'But never mind.'

'It will take blood,' said Thurza, glancing at him. 'Blood was spilled to call the Gorm before. This stone you call St Chyan's Chair ain't no chair at all. 'Tis an altar, and blood was spilled here for the Gorm.'

'Sadly, we have none about us,' said Will. 'Would wine do? There is some cheap claret in the pantry . . .'

Thurza hissed at him. The fire settled, tossing a shower of sparks into the darkening sky. Westward, the sun was sinking into a band of thick cloud, which Utterly was certain had not been there before. The roar of the breakers came loudly from below. 'You mock me,' the sea-witch growled, 'but there'll be no mockery left in 'ee once the Gorm rises. And rise it will. Blood will call it, and we have blood in plenty. It runs in the veins of that sea-got child, that tide-washed thing you call a girl.'

Her finger, pale and knobbly and slightly trembling, pointed straight at Utterly. Her fire-cast shadow danced upon the turf. The old stones seemed to lean in towards the flames, glad of a chance to warm themselves again after all those fireless centuries.

'Enough, Mrs Froy,' said Will sternly. 'I'll not have you calling Utterly such names.'

'I'll do more than call her names,' the sea-witch shouted. 'I'll slit her open and let her blood go a-dribbling down into the waves, and then we shall see what rises to our bait!'

'It was a mistake to bring you here,' said Will. 'You should leave now. This experiment is over.' He turned to call to Mrs Skraeveling. 'Would you take Utterly back into the house, Mrs S?'

'Uncle Will!' screamed Utterly, at the same moment that Mrs Skraeveling cried out, 'Master Will!' Their two voices blended almost like a song.

She was strong, that old witch. Maybe it was the sea air that had kept her so tough and sinewy all these years. Ancient as she was, she could still move quickly when she wished to. The instant Will had turned to speak to Mrs Skraeveling, she'd snatched up one of the shipwreck timbers she had discarded from the fire and swung it at his head so hard that Utterly heard the crack even over the bellowing of the sea.

Uncle Will sprawled on his face in the grass. The witch sprang over him, dropping the timber and pulling from her skirts a jagged old carving knife with a driftwood handle. She snatched Utterly by the wrist, pulled her away from Mrs Skraeveling, and held the blade against her neck while she shouted, 'You leave me be! She is the Gorm's by rights, and if 'ee try and come between the Gorm and that which is the Gorm's, I'll slice 'ee down!'

Mrs Skraeveling took a hesitant step towards her, wary of the knife. Thurza pushed the cold blade harder against Utterly's neck and Utterly squeaked in fear. 'Skraeveling!' shouted Mrs Skraeveling, but her husband was halfway down the cliff track, off on his quest to fetch the vicar.

Thurza Froy made a gargling sound that might have been her laughter, but it was hard to be sure, because the sea was roaring so, the wind was wuthering around the stones, and from the west, like a roll of kettledrums, came the first long grumble of thunder as the storm cleared its throat. The sea-witch dragged Utterly into the circle of stones, into the heat of the fire. She flung her, face down, across St Chyan's Chair. Utterly saw for the first time that the surface of the old stone had been carved with wave-patterns, and that it had a groove cut in its edge for blood to flow down, like a butcher's slab.

'Sea, rise!' screamed Thurza Froy, setting one bony knee on Utterly's back to hold her down. She raised both hands to the sky, the knife bright with firelight and the first blue-white flaring of the storm. 'Waves, roll!' she shrieked, and the waves seemed to hear her, pounding and pounding at the cliff's feet.

Utterly lifted her head. Above the western sea the sky was all storm, a wall of darkness toppling towards her. But on the horizon a dim red bar of light showed where the sun was setting, and outlined against it she could see the Hidden Lands, hidden no more but very clear and seeming quite close.

Will saw them too. He opened his eyes to find Mrs Skraeveling stooped over him sobbing, 'Oh, Master Will, she will murder her!' while gulls blew by on the wind with long, despairing cries and the sea-witch in the distance somewhere howled, 'Great Gorm, come, eat up the land!' Will turned his head, astonished at the pain that caused him, and there were the islands, black and definite against the blood-red west as if they had risen from the depths to prove him wrong.

'Mrs Skraeveling,' he said, 'I think I have been a very great fool.'

'Master Will, she is murdering our Utterly!' wailed Mrs Skraeveling.

Through the pale flames of the driftwood fire, Will saw Thurza Froy with her knife held high, and Utterly trapped and squirming on the stone. He got to his feet, but the pain in his head and the wind howling across the clifftop bent him double. He grabbed a discarded length of driftwood and passed it to Mrs Skraeveling. 'I will distract her,' he said, 'and you must snatch Utterly to safety . . .'

'Sea, rise! Waves, roll!' chanted Thurza Froy, swaying to and fro as if she were trying to hypnotize the sea, or perhaps herself. Pinned under the witch's knee, Utterly twisted round and saw Mrs Skraeveling advancing on one side, clutching her makeshift club, while Uncle Will edged forward on the other. She made herself go very still and quiet, hoping the sea-witch would be too caught up in her spells to look behind and see what they were planning.

But in the end it did not matter, because the sea had plans of its own. There was a startling triple-flash of lightning, and by its glare Utterly saw that the waves were moving in some new and unhealthy way, like a pan of thick broth coming quickly to the boil. She had seen the sea move like that before, in dark dreams she had forgotten. They came rushing back to her now. She knew what was about to happen.

'It is here!' she screamed.

The wind gusted. The fire laid flat upon the ground and growled. Thurza Froy stopped her chant. The sea-witch cowered back, appalled at the success of her spells. Utterly seized her chance and rolled sideways off St Chyan's Chair and down onto the turf, where Mrs Skraeveling snatched her by one hand and dragged her clear.

'We must get away from the stones,' Utterly shouted.

Uncle Will did not ask why. He picked her up and

177

started to carry her quickly back towards the lights of Sundown Watch. Mrs Skraeveling went with them. As they hurried along the treacherous path Utterly looked back over her uncle's shoulder to see if Thurza Froy was chasing them. But the witch was still standing by her fire, her face turned towards the sea, slowly lowering her knife as if she had forgotten why she'd brought it with her in the first place.

'It has come at my call!' she shouted, sounding amazed. 'It has come at my call!'

A low-tide stench of rot and ooze broke over the headland like an invisible wave. The thunder spoke again, right overhead. Lightning burst across the sky, and Utterly saw that the sea was being shouldered aside by something that was rising from beneath it.

She had tried so many times to imagine the Gorm. She had pictured it as a serpent, a great fish, a sea dragon, even that moth-eaten mer-lion from the painting in the dining room. She had imagined it as big as a horse, as big as an elephant, as big as a whale. And all her imaginings had been entirely wrong.

For the Gorm was as big as the sea. It was as tall as the sky. It was as if all the weed that ever grew in the vast deeps west of Wildsea had uprooted itself at once and massed itself somehow into this: a lumbering, shapeless thing with countless limbs. It was so big that it seemed impossible to believe in it even when you were looking right at it; even when the lightning came crackling down to crown its lumpish head with a wreath of St Elmo's fire.

'My God!' shouted Uncle Will, hearing Utterly's cry and turning to see what had alarmed her. Mrs Skraeveling went hurrying on ahead of them in a flurry of panic and petticoats, but Uncle Will stopped running, and Utterly clung to his neck, and they both stared at the Gorm as it reached out something too boneless and too huge to call a hand and slammed it down upon St Chyan's Head, blotting out the fire, scattering the old megaliths like ninepins.

Glistening tentacle-fingers spread and flexed and tightened. Rocks burst apart, cracks zigzagged up the cliffs, the headland groaned and toppled. Utterly glimpsed Thurza Froy scuttling across the tilting summit like a frightened spider, then lost sight of her amid the plunging fragments, the white foam bursting upward, the waterfalls cascading down the weed-wall of the Gorm's flank as it turned.

'Run!' she wailed, and Will ran, following Mrs Skraeveling back up the lawn towards the house. Still watching over his shoulder, Utterly saw the Gorm throw back the shapeless, eyeless thing that served it for a head and roar, and the sea cave of its mouth was lined with teeth, and every tooth was the wreck of a sunken ship.

26

THE GORMBLADE

Will set Utterly down on the back doorstep and flung wide the door. She fled into the house, although she knew the house would be no shelter. Something that could pull down St Chyan's Head could crush Sundown Watch like an eggshell.

She ran to her room and looked out of the window there. The Gorm had shrunk a little, or perhaps the miles of weed it must be made from had gathered themselves tighter, so that water squeezed out of it and poured down its flanks and crashed back whitely into the sea. At any rate, it seemed no bigger than a large-ish mountain now.

It was still just as terrifying though. New limbs reached out of it and then withdrew, as if it could not decide whether to shape itself into a squid or a jellyfish or a giant human being.

It leaned over the cliffs and peered at Sundown Watch, and Utterly backed away from the window. It made an irritable movement, a kind of swiping gesture with a handful of its hands, and Utterly shut her eyes as the whole house shook. There was a rush of falling masonry, a crash of splintered beams, the sleigh-bell tinkle of broken glass. But the house remained standing, or at least Utterly's part of it did, and when she looked again the Gorm was moving away, shambling over the shards of the torn-down headland and creeping south along the shore.

Uncle Will came in. In the dim light from the window his face was the colour of old snow. 'Utterly, I am so sorry,' he said. He stood with her at the window and they watched the giant shape go stamping through the deeps of Belfriars Bay with the waves bursting around its many feet. 'Utterly,' he said, 'you are right, you were right all along . . .'

Utterly was not so pleased to hear him say it as she had thought she would be. She wished she had been wrong. She wished he had been right, and the Gorm was just old stories. Old stories could not tear down cliffs, could they?

'Uncle Will,' she said, 'I think it has knocked down our Tower.'

'It is all my fault,' said Uncle Will. 'I made the sea-witch

181

call it, and it answered her call . . .' He reached behind his head and touched the place where Thurza Froy had hit him, then studied the blood on his hand by stormlight.

Thunder crashed. The Gorm bellowed. Like the sea, it seemed to have no particular plan in mind. Like a child in a tantrum, it was driven by feelings, not by any thought. It raged down the coast as far as the Spillikins, kicked a few seastacks over as if they were sandcastles, then turned and started back.

'I must stop it,' said Will. 'I am Watcher. It is my duty to stop it.'

Utterly followed him through the dark house to the dining room. Lightning threw quick white window-shapes across the walls and lit up the painting of the Gorm, which now looked quite a friendly, cuddly sort of Gorm compared to the one bellowing outside. Mrs Skraeveling came in, recommending bandages, ointment and a nice sit-down. 'That nasty witch caught you such a crack on the head, Master Will,' she said. 'You must pull up a chair and sit a while.'

Uncle Will pulled up a chair, but did not sit. He placed the chair against the wall beside the fireplace and stood on it to fetch down the first Watcher's sword. The Gormblade gleamed dimly under its layers of dust as lightning blinked in at the windows. Thin cobwebs trailed from it. 'I suppose I should have had it sharpened,' Will said.

Utterly thought of suggesting Mr Skraeveling's gun instead, but she could not see how a gun would be any more use against the Gorm than the sword. She could not see how a troop of horse artillery would be any use against something so big and angry as the Gorm.

'It feels rather like taking a toothpick to attack a charging elephant, doesn't it?' Uncle Will said ruefully, when he saw her watching him. 'The Gorm will no more be harmed by it than we are harmed when we are bitten by an ant.'

'It is supposed to be a *magic* sword,' said Utterly, though she was thinking how un-magical it looked.

'And if an ant bit me hard enough,' said Mrs Skraeveling, 'I might decide to go away and have my picnic somewhere else.'

Another furious bellow shook the house. It came from the landward side this time. It seemed the Gorm had grown bored of stomping seastacks, and found its way ashore. They all ran through to the hallway and Utterly peeked out past her uncle as he opened the front door. It was night-dark in the garden, and when the lightning flashed Utterly saw the air was full of snow, huge white flakes of it twirling like dancers as they rode the breeze and settled lightly on the shrubbery. It was not really snow, though; just sea foam blown inland on the storm. Behind the falling flakes an immense darkness was moving slowly north across St Chyan's Common.

'Oh, my Lord, it will be making for Marazea!' gasped Mrs Skraeveling.

'We shall see about that,' said Uncle Will, gripping his ridiculous sword more tightly, and he stepped out into the swirl of sea-snow, into the brief, flinching brightness of the lightning.

'Uncle Will!' shouted Utterly.

'Look after Mrs Skraeveling for me,' he called, as he ran across the garden. 'Mrs Skraeveling, look after Utterly!'

'Uncle Will!' shouted Utterly again. She wanted to go with him, but he was already at the gate and through it, and then Mrs Skraeveling was pulling her back inside the house and shutting the door. A few flakes of foam came inside with them as it closed, and settled gently on the hall rug.

'I will not lock it,' said Mrs Skraeveling, 'because no lock will keep the Gorm out, and what if my Skraeveling comes home and wants to get in? I sent him to fetch Reverend Dearlove. Oh, I do hope that old Gorm has not stomped him flat!'

❖

Mr Skraeveling had not been stomped flat yet. As Will ran down the cliff track with his sword, a long stutter of lightning showed him two figures a little way ahead.

184

When he drew close he saw that they were Mr Skraeveling and Reverend Dearlove. They had been hurrying back from the vicarage, and had stopped dumbstruck on the road to watch the Gorm.

Dearlove turned at the sound of Will's footsteps. In the blackness between lightning flashes he was visible chiefly by the white bands of his collar. 'Will!' he shouted 'What did you do? You have raised Leviathan! This is the End of Days!'

'The vicar's a bit upset,' explained Mr Skraeveling, running to meet Will. 'Mrs Skraeveling sent me to fetch him, thinking he could stop old Thurza stirring up her mischief, but it seems 'tis a bit too late for that.'

Dearlove raised his arms, and raised his voice too, trying to outshout the thunder. Fragments of his words blew past Will on the wind, mingled with sea foam and the vast dank stench of the Gorm. *I stood upon the sand of the sea, and saw a beast rise up out of the sea!* the vicar yelled. *And upon his horns ten crowns, and upon his heads the name of blasphemy!*

'Calm yourself, man!' Will shouted. 'There's nothing you can do at Sundown Watch. Go back to the vicarage and look to Mrs Dearlove and the children. Mr Skraeveling, Utterly and your wife are safe at the house . . .'

'I'll see they stay that way, sir,' said Mr Skraeveling, and hurried on up the track while Will grabbed Dearlove by the wet broadcloth of his coat and started towing

185

him downhill. At the foot of the cliff, where the path branched towards the dunes and the lights of the vicarage, Will told him again to go back to his family, gave him a shove to set him on his way, then ran on alone. Ahead, where the lights of Marazea should be, there was only darkness, and the Gorm. It had grown more human-shaped, Will thought. From its head, way up there in the scudding cloud-base, yards-long streamers of kelp blew out on the gale like a woman's hair. It reminded Will of that curious list of names his brother had scribbled in the Log. *Thalassa, Tethys, Tiamat, the Gorm . . .*

It turned, as if it could feel Will coming. Perhaps by some sorcery it had sensed the blade he held. Or perhaps it had simply seen the gleam of metal. The ground lurched. A sudden hill appeared in Will's way, barring the track to Marazea. The hill was one of the Gorm's feet, woven from twined ropes of underwater weed, all groaning and creaking and stretching as the Gorm's weight shifted. Shards of rock jutted out of the weed like random talons. Torrents of seawater spilled down the Gorm's legs, and rained in white cataracts from the bulk of its body high above.

It is so very big, thought Will, and I am so small. Its smell reminded him of his terror of the sea caves he had explored with Drewe when he was just a boy, afraid of the dark, afraid of the incoming tide, afraid of imagined monsters, afraid of being called a coward. He felt no older or stronger or more capable of dealing with this thing now than he would have been then. But he knew that was how other young men must have felt before him, facing the French at Corunna or Austerlitz, so he did what he presumed they must have done: remembered his duty, said his prayers, shouted a shrill, wordless, terrified war cry, and charged straight at his enemy.

27

THE DUNES

In Sundown Watch the candles flickered, their flames dragged sideways by the wind that found its way through the gaps in the shutters. The old house creaked like a ship in high seas, and the chimneys moaned. But at least Mr Skraeveling was home now, though drenched with spray and trembly from the things he had seen on the way.

'Mr Dark will set things right,' said Mrs Skraeveling, trying her best to sound as if she believed it.

'I still don't see why old Thurza's bonfire should annoy it so,' said her husband.

But it wasn't the fire, thought Utterly, watching them talk. It wasn't the fire and it wasn't the words that made the Gorm rise. It has been watching all the while, I could feel it. But it was only when Thurza promised it blood that it came. And it can't have been the blood itself it wanted, because she hadn't time to cut me, so it was just the mention of it . . .

And she suddenly saw things as they must have looked to the Gorm, as it lurked there in the western sea with its attention concentrated on the tableau unfolding between the old stones.

Thurza Froy doesn't understand the Gorm at all, she thought. It didn't come because she called it. It thought I was in danger. It came to stop her harming me!

That made her feel very important, but also very frightened. She could not imagine why the Gorm should care about her so, nor what it might do next in its efforts to protect her.

❖

The blade drove deep into the Gorm's foot, and jarred Will's shoulders damnably as it struck against some boulder buried there. The Gorm shrieked, a noise like shrill thunder high overhead. It sounded more like rage than pain. It drew back its foot, as a man might who had jabbed his toe upon an unseen pin. How could it have felt the sword? Will wondered. But then how could it see, move, make noises? How could it exist at all? Nothing about the Gorm made that sort of sense. He lunged with the sword again, but the creature had snatched its foot away, and he tumbled face first into the deep pit of its footprint.

The Gorm stooped, swinging the matted moon of its great head to and fro as if scanning the ground for the bug which had stung it. Light jumped from the sky and glittered in ten thousand eyes, which were really ten thousand shards of sea-worn glass stuck where a face should be. The mouth, half open, showed its shipwreck teeth. Sheets of salt water fell on Will till he was as wet as he had been when he was shipwrecked. Fish squeezed from the Gorm's coils flapped on the earth around him. Spluttering, he scrambled up out of the Gorm's footprint and stuck the sword into it again.

Again it snatched its foot away, and this time most of the sword went with it, wedged in the tangles of weed, leaving only the snapped-off hilt in Will's grasp. 'No!' he shouted, and the Gorm heard him. He ran from it as fast as he could towards the dunes, flinging the sword-hilt aside. Weaponless, he felt his only hope was to lead it back towards the sea and away from Sundown Watch and all the other huddled homes of Wildsea.

The Gorm let out its thunder-shriek again, and swung down a ponderous fist. It would have smashed Will flat, except that a lightning flash showed him the black shadow swelling on the earth around him and he threw himself sideways just before it struck. The ground trembled. Massive feet slammed down around Will, then slowly moved away. He stood up, slipped, somersaulted downhill through briars and small bushes into a sodden hollow full of toppled walls and smashed timber and the flapping muslin ghosts of curtains. It was the ruins of the vicarage.

'Dearlove?' Will shouted, looking about him in horror as he realized where he was. 'Mrs Dearlove? Children?'

There was no answer – only the thunder, and the rolling broadsides of the breakers in the bay. Had Dearlove come home as Will had told him to? Was he lying smothered underneath all this wreckage, or had only his wife and children been at home when the Gorm came calling?

Lightning played across the rubble. Looking up, Will saw the Gorm. He remembered his scheme of leading it back to the sea. He had failed the Dearloves, but he might still save the rest of Marazea. 'Here!' he shouted, at the top of his voice. 'Here I am!'

The eyes of the Gorm flashed with electric reflections as it turned towards the tiny sound of Will's challenge. Terror took him and he ran seaward, the shards of Mrs Dearlove's best dinner service crunching under his feet, then mud and scattered beanpoles, grass, and at last the wet sand of the backs of the dunes. He scrambled up them, slither-stumbling as the sand gave way and slid beneath him, grasping at thin clumps of windswept marram grass to drag himself to the summit. Ahead lay the sea, a procession of whitecaps rolling landward to break in white smoke and a sound of cannonfire. He turned again to make sure the Gorm was following, and found it was closer than he had thought.

A limb lashed down, and the dune where he was standing burst apart. He was in the air, along with half a ton of sand and a cataract of clammy weed. The sea turned somersaults; the Gorm bellowed; Will screamed. Then he struck the ground, and half Marazea beach came thudding down to bury him.

❖

Thurza Froy was surprisingly hard to kill. When the Gorm ripped St Chyan's Head apart, she thought her end had come, but the splinter of cliff that she was clinging to struck against another as it fell, and toppling sideways smashed against a piece that was still standing, and tumbled Thurza off onto the grass at the edge of Sundown Watch's lawn. She lay there dazed a while, listening to the sea crash and the Gorm rampage.

So it had come at last, to trample and drown her fellow islanders! Although she had always told them that it would, Thurza felt surprised. All these years she had been saying her spells and lighting her fires and making her dark promises to the Gorm, and now the Gorm had finally responded she found she had never really believed it would come.

She stood up and looked around. St Chyan's Head was gone, and fierce white waves were bickering over the fragments of it. Sundown Watch had suffered too: she was pleased to see the Gorm had demolished the Tower and the whole southern end of the house. Rubble littered the lawns, and one of the fallen semaphore arms had skewered Mr Skraeveling's potting shed.

Looking north, she made out the pale surf in St Chyan's bay, and then lightning showed her the Gorm. She heard it bellow. It looked liable to trample Wildsea so flat that the waves would roll over the whole island as if it were no more than a sandbar at high tide. Thurza wanted to be riding those waves, not underneath them. Besides, the Hidden Lands had showed themselves. If she could get back to her own hut and the boat which waited on the beach below it, she could sail there. While the Gorm was busy with its vengeance, she would creep into its mansions and find her Davey, and all the treasures she had sent him diving for . . .

She scurried around the side of the house, crossed the garden, and found that part of the wall had tumbled down, allowing her to scramble over it and out onto the cliff track. Reasoning that the Gorm would be busy inland, she made for the beach, meaning to follow it north to the Undercliff where her boat was waiting.

How she would launch it off this lee shore, against this gale, she did not know, but she had faith in her own cleverness. Old Thurza would find a way.

Lightning split the sky above her as she scrambled over the dunes, and she sensed things moving there, and froze. It was Men o' Weed, a small army of them, going past her in the dark with lolloping boneless strides and a soft sea-symphony of slithering and squelching sounds. Thurza dropped out of sight. She had not outwitted death only to be finished off by those sorry, staggering scarecrows. Crouching in the thin grass, she kept very still as the ragged silhouettes went slouching by and started up the track to Sundown Watch.

28

THE SIEGE OF
SUNDOWN WATCH

'Dark? Will Dark?' Strong fingers found Will's face, and started scooping aside the wet sand which had buried him. He struggled a sandy hand free and wiped his sandy eyes. There was a veil of silver upon the sky above him: a brief sliver of moonlight under the black skirts of the storm. Silhouetted against it was a terrifying, antlered head.

'Will Dark,' it said, 'whenever you are not being drowned, you are being buried alive. You are the unluckiest man I ever met.'

'Miss Aish!' said Will, hoping she had not noticed the girlish shriek he had let out when he first saw her. Now that he knew who she was, he found that he had never been so glad to see anyone. She leaned down and hugged him, hauling him out of his sandy grave with his face pressed into the tangle of trinkets strung around her neck. The smell of her, like warm wet earth, seemed an antidote to the estuarine stench of the Gorm. 'Pardon me,' he said, 'It was the antlers. I mistook you for a devil, or a hobgoblin . . .'

'I did not think you believed in such things?'

'I did not believe in the Gorm, and that has turned out to be real enough,' Will said, flinching as its awful roar came echoing across the dunes. 'Perhaps all such things are real. I owe you an apology. I have been a very great fool.'

'Well, at least you know it now,' said Aish. 'I saw your white hand sticking up. But for that, I'd not have found you. Egg came running to tell me what was happening. I came as fast as I could, but it was not fast enough. The Gorm has found her way ashore far sooner than I thought.'

'It was all my fault,' said Will, feeling horribly ashamed. 'I made the sea-witch summon it.'

Aish gave a sceptical snort. 'The Gorm does not answer to Thurza Froy, nor to you, Will Dark. She would have come sooner or later, called or not. She has been thinking about coming for a year and more. I have felt her eyes on us, and seen the Hidden Lands.'

'So you told me. So Utterly told me, and I did not listen to her either. Now Dearlove's place is in ruins, and

196

it was I who sent him back there. They are all dead, Mrs Dearlove and her poor children – and all because I am a fool.'

'Everyone is a fool sometimes,' said Aish, helping him to stand. 'Your worst folly was running out to face her all alone. But that is not your fault. The Watchers have forgotten that old John Dark had help in his battle with her all those years ago.'

Will took off his boots and tipped sand out of them. 'In the old tale,' he said, 'John Dark was aided by a guardian spirit of the island. But that is just a legend . . .'

'As was the Gorm, till she came out of the sea and started knocking people's houses flat,' said Aish. 'John Dark's old sword was not ever enough to cut her down. It needs spells said over it. My land magic may not be as grand as her sea magic, but I can put power in a blade enough to stop her rampages for a while.'

'Then are you . . . ?' Will said, and could not quite bring himself to ask the thing he was wondering. She glanced at him, and though it was pitch-dark Will saw a gleam of light deep in her eyes, the colour of sunlight in a peat-stream.

'Now where is your sword, Watcher?' she asked. 'Buried hereabouts, I suppose. We shall dig it up like a dog finding a bone, and I shall say my little words over it, and then you may go and teach old Mistress Gorm her manners.'

She sounded so wholly in control of things that Will actually found himself looking around, half expecting the Gormblade to rise out of the sand like Excalibur. It took him a moment to remember.

'It is gone!' he said. 'The blade broke off, and I cast the hilt aside. It is' – he gestured hopelessly at the darkness inland – 'it is somewhere between here and the track.'

Away towards Marazea, dogs were barking. The Gorm roared and hooted. Aish stood silently for a moment.

'All right, Will Dark,' she said, 'then we are in a pickle.'

❖

At Sundown Watch the drawing room shutters rattled as if something more than the storm was trying to get in. Utterly and the Skraevelings looked at the windows, then at each other.

'It is only the wind,' said Mr Skraeveling, sounding very certain. But he stood up anyway and hurried off to fetch his gun.

He had no sooner left the room than the crack and tinkle of a broken pane came from behind the shutters, and then another, and the shutters themselves bowed inwards under a blow that sounded more as if it was struck by a fist than by the wild west wind.

'Get behind me, kitten,' said Mrs Skraeveling, picking up a poker from the fireplace. Utterly did as she was told.

She wished she had a poker too, but she had to make do with the tongs.

The shutters bowed again, and this time the latch that held them closed broke off and they slammed open. Behind them, dark tangled clumps of weed were being forced in through the broken windowpanes. They tumbled down onto the window sill and onto the floor below it, writhed there, and then reared up, reassembling themselves at startling speed into a Man o' Weed which came lurching towards Utterly. Behind it, another was already forcing its way in.

Utterly screamed and backed away. She could not help herself. She told herself the Gorm had only wanted to protect her, and these creatures were its friends or servants and must want the same, but they did not look friendly, not with those faceless faces and those out-stretched, grasping paws.

'Oh no you don't, you creature!' said Mrs Skraeveling, and struck the advancing weed-man such a blow that its head came halfway off and both its glass eyes fell out and dropped on the hearth rug. It crumpled to its knees and started groping for them, while Utterly and Mrs Skraeveling moved towards the door and Mrs Skraeveling shouted, 'Jan!'

The door burst open just as they reached it. Mr Skraeveling, entering with the gun, said, 'Lord save us!' and shot the second Man o' Weed as it came lumbering across the room. The room filled with smoke and noise. The impact of the lead ball sent the Man o' Weed staggering back a pace or two, but seemed to do it no other harm. It came shambling on again with flakes of half-burned wadding smouldering in the entanglements of its chest. Behind it the second had found one of its eyes and wedged it Cyclops-fashion in the centre of its clumsily re-woven head. A third was oozing its way in through the window.

'Come,' shouted Mr Skraeveling, and he began bundling Utterly and his wife ahead of him out of the room. But other Men o' Weed had found their way in through other windows: two were lurching along the passageway from the direction of Utterly's bedroom, and another was creeping down the stairs, smearing its clumsy wet hands over the carved tortoise on the landing newel post.

From the hallway came a thudding sound as something wet and soft and heavy threw itself against the front door.

29

SEA MAGIC, LAND MAGIC

When she was sure the Men o' Weed were gone, Thurza crept out of her hiding place and went down onto the beach. It seemed to her the wind was slackening. Patches of moonlight chased across the sand. The storm would be over by the time she reached her boat, she thought, and she looked seaward to make sure the islands were still out there.

In the breaking surf a figure stood, so shapeless she thought at first it was another of those pesty Men o' Weed. But lightning obligingly lit up the beach just then, and by its glare she saw the stranger's body was topped with a tall cone, as if a shark had sprouted arms and legs and walked up on land with its snout pointed at the sky. The round glass windows of its eyes flashed lightning at her.

'Davey?' whispered Thurza, as it left the surf and stalked towards her up the sand.

For she knew that sealskin form, with its mitten paws and towering hood, and the lead-soled feet it lifted and set down so awkwardly at every step. She had stitched the careful seams of it herself, and when it drew closer, wading through a pool of moonlight, she thought she could see her own thumbprints in the tar that sealed the edges of its eyeholes.

'My Davey-boy!' she giggled girlishly. 'You come back to me! You have saved me a voyage to them Hidden Lands! Tell me you've brought some o' the Gorm's treasures home with you . . .'

The diver showed no sign of having heard. The awful thought crept into Thurza's head that Davey might not recognize her. Years had gone by since the white lady of the Hidden Lands had stolen him away, and perhaps time passed slower in the Mansions of the Gorm. For all Thurza knew, it did not pass at all. Her Davey might be a young man still, and not recognize this old woman who stood waiting for him on the beach. She patted nervously at the filthy white tangles of her hair. She pulled the rotting crab from around her neck and tossed it aside, hoping he had not noticed it.

The diver loomed over her in the moonlight. She looked into the suit's eyepieces, yearning for a glimpse of Davey's own dear handsome face, but mist or mildew coated the inside of the glass. Through the seams around them, water oozed out like salt tears.

'Take off that old hood, Davey-boy,' said Thurza, and raised her wrinkled old face to be kissed.

Poor Thurza Froy. All those years of waiting, all those years of watching, all those years of pondering on the legends of the Gorm, and still she had never really understood it. She believed it was one creature, and that its Men o' Weed and the white lady who had taken a fancy to her Davey were just its servants. She did not understand the weed-men and the lady *were* the Gorm, and that the Gorm inhabited them in the same way it inhabited the towering thing now stamping barns and fences flat behind her. She did not understand that the white lady had not taken a fancy to her Davey, but only to his diving suit. She did not understand it was the cold mind of the Gorm which looked down at her now through those discs of bottle-bottom glass. She did not understand it was the Gorm's hands that seized her like vices and began to drag her down the beach. She did not understand that the Gorm was also in the tall white wave which came rolling in to bury her, and in the cold salt water which prised her teeth apart and gurgled down her throat and filled her lungs.

Poor Thurza Froy. There were so many things she had not understood. And now it was too late.

❖

Will and Aish stumbled down the dunes onto the flat, grassy land behind. Two shaggy ponies waited there, and on the back of one Will saw Egg, holding the halter of the second pony. Both animals were terrified, their eyes showing white in the smears of moonlight which kept racing over them. Egg talked steadily to them to keep them from bolting. 'Hush now, hush there, what's to fear, look, herself is here . . .' He gave Will Dark a hard stare when he came near, to let him know *he* blamed him for this ballyhoo, even if Aish didn't.

'Egg,' said Aish, 'do you have your hunting spear with you?'

Of course he had! Egg wasn't stupid enough to venture out unarmed on this haunted night, with weed-men and what-have-you creeping everywhere. It was strapped across his back in the sling he'd made for it. He slipped it off, and passed it to Aish. The shaft was an ash pole, not quite straight. Moonlight trickled over the sharp edges of the stone blade.

'Made it myself,' he told Will.

'Can we harm the Gorm with that?' asked Will.

'Its blade is upland stone,' said Aish, and shrugged. 'It will have some land magic in it. We can but try.' She spat on the spearhead, rubbed the saliva into it, whispered words Will did not recognize. Then, glancing at Egg, she said, 'You take the ponies now, and go up with them to Sundown Watch.'

'But I want to come with you!' Egg said. 'It is my spear,' he added sulkily.

'But we must go right up to the Gorm to use it, and you are too useful to be trodden on. Off with you to the Watch now, and look after Utterly. We shall come and find you there.'

'If *you* ain't trodden on,' said Egg. He sounded sullen and close to tears, but Aish gave him a meaningful look and he turned his pony about and rode off leading the other. Both animals seemed glad to be moving away from the Gorm, and went as fast as Egg would let them. He vanished into the darkness, shouting to them to slow down.

Aish handed the spear to Will. 'Now we must get close enough to her so you can use it,' she said.

❖

'Oh, Jan, whatever shall we do?' whispered Mrs Skraeveling as the Men o' Weed advanced. They were not fast, but they showed no sign of stopping. They were as patient as the incoming tide.

'I'll hold them off, Carrie,' said Mr Skraeveling bravely. 'You get young Utterly out through the kitchen if you can, and run and hide out on the common.'

'No!' said Utterly.

''Twill be all right, kitten,' said Mrs Skraeveling

unconvincingly, taking Utterly firmly by one hand. But a clatter of falling pans told Utterly the Men o' Weed had already found a way into the kitchen, and anyway, she could not leave Mr Skraeveling to face them on his own. Besides, she did not think it was the Skraevelings they were interested in. She had the same feeling she had often had before, that the eyes of the sea were upon her. The feeling was as strong as the low-tide reek of weed which filled the house, blotting out all the familiar scents of home.

She put her hands over her ears so she could think. This was what Aish had spoken of, the long war between the land and sea, only now it had become an actual war, and people she loved were going to be hurt in the fighting. But if she was right and the Gorm was seeking to protect her, then she was the cause of it all. And if she was the cause, then she could end it, by just giving the Gorm what it wanted.

'Now then, cully,' said Mr Skraeveling, swinging his empty gun like a cudgel at the nearest Man o' Weed. But the Man o' Weed had no nose to break, no skull to crack. The gun-butt thudding into its head did not trouble it any more than had all the rocks and boulders it must have been bashed against as it made its slimy way ashore. It lifted Mr Skraeveling up in its greasy paws and flung him like a doll against the wall.

That settled it. Utterly knew she had to do something

to stop this, before the Men o' Weed killed Mr Skraeveling, and the Gorm stomped all of Wildsea flat. She twisted her hand free of Mrs Skraeveling's and ran through the hall towards the front door. 'Leave them alone!' she shouted. 'I am here! I am coming!'

'Utterly!' wailed Mrs Skraeveling.

'It is all right!' Utterly told her. 'They have come for me. If I go with them, they will trouble you no more.'

She hoped she was right.

When she opened the door, the weed-man who had been throwing himself against it was taken by surprise and tumbled through onto the doormat. Utterly jumped over the slithering heap of him and ran out into the garden.

The dozen Men o' Weed who stood there turned their heads to look at her, and the six who had followed her through the house gathered behind her in the doorway.

Utterly felt frightened, but not as frightened as she thought she would feel. She made a slightly trembly curtsey. 'Well, here I am,' she said. 'I will come with you, if you leave my friends alone.'

The Men o' Weed encircled her. Utterly was not sure if they had heard her words, or understood them. Did they even have ears? Did they even have brains? Passing moonlight brushed them with silver and lit cold sparks in the glass of their eyes. One reached out to Utterly, and then drew his hand back as if she had burned him.

Utterly put a hand up to her neck and felt the hairy string of Aish's green stone pendant there, and the bump of the stone itself where it hung inside the collar of her dress. She pulled it out. The weed-men rustled, and she felt a thrill of relief, knowing that the pendant would protect her from them. But beyond them another moonbeam shone on Marazea and she saw the Gorm there, stamping on something, throwing its head back to give a howl that rolled across the island and echoed off the hills.

With both hands she carefully lifted the pendant off over her head, and held it out at arm's length. The Men o' Weed watched expectantly. If they had breath, they would have held it. Utterly opened her fingers and let the green stone drop. She heard the small noise as it fell quite clearly, for the wind which had been moaning around the corners of the house suddenly died. Even the sea was quiet. The Gorm had stopped its bellowing. For a moment all was still, and in the stillness Utterly thought she heard the hoof beats of horses coming fast up the track from Marazea.

Then the Men o' Weed closed in on her, wrapping strong kelp-stalk fingers around her, lifting her gently off her feet. And down in Blanchmane's Cove the sea woke up again, and the waves roared out in triumph, '*Utterly!*'

30

VICTORY AND DEFEAT

William and Aish went north, through scrub and rough
pasture. Ahead of them the Gorm loomed and
hooted. It appeared to be trampling down the dunes near
Marazea. Perhaps it was stamping out a channel through
which the waves could spill to flood the fields and farms
behind. Or perhaps in its elemental fury it just wanted to
boot huge piles of sand about.

'You refer to it as "she",' Will said, finding that talking
took the edge off his terror. 'As if it is a woman . . .'

'I reckon anything so strong and clever and so prone
to hold a grudge must be,' Aish replied. 'Men are simple
creatures, and much easier to handle.'

'But what is she? A thing of weed and shipwrecks . . .'

'She is the sea's dream of itself,' said Aish. 'She woke

up when the first storm howled across the face of the first ocean. She has other shapes. A different shape for every mood. This one is what her anger looks like.'

And I am the one who angered her, thought Will, and wondered why the Gorm had not smashed Sundown Watch as flat as the dunes she was trampling now, or made a point of finding him. He weighed Egg's spear in his hands. Small as it was, it seemed well-balanced, but he had never thrown a spear before. He looked up at the Gorm, then back at Aish, recalling the strength of her hug, her strong huntress's arms.

He held out the spear to her. 'You must do it!'

'You are Watcher.'

The Gorm boomed like surf on a lee shore. It was not far from them now. The stench of it filled the air and made it hard to speak or think. One of its legs barred the way ahead like a fortress. Will readied his little spear.

'Gorm!' Aish shouted. 'Old Gorm! Old weed-wight! Old sea's fury! Look down here! Look what we have for thee! It is a blade of good stone from the heart of my land. Will you have a taste of it?'

Will flung the spear, and lost sight of it in the darkness as soon as it had left his hand. He supposed it had found its mark and buried itself in the Gorm's entanglements. He waited for a sign that it had done some harm, but all that happened was a sudden silence. Even the wind was stilled. Even the sea was quiet.

The Gorm turned round with an immense twisting and slithering rearrangement of itself, a tightening and slackening of the long hawsers of kelp which muscled it, until it was facing Aish and Will. The moonlight raced over it and Will marvelled again at how huge and awful it was. Now it will trample us both, he thought. Perhaps Aish was thinking the same, for she reached for his hand at the same moment he reached for hers. There they stood like frightened children, awaiting their punishment.

But the Gorm was not looking at them. Its gaze was directed over them, back towards Sundown Watch and the ruins of St Chyan's head. And as they stood watching, it seemed to sag, and then swiftly began to lose its shape, and fell in upon itself like a tower undermined, crumpling and crumbling, melting into an avalanche of weed which would have buried Will all over again if Aish had not shouted for him to run.

They ran, and the noise of the Gorm's collapse filled the air with a rushing roar like the voices of the fountains of the deep. When at last they stopped on a dune-top and turned, gasping, to look back, the land and the beach behind them were unrecognizable: a wasteland of weed-mountains in the moonlight, littered with the hulks of long-lost ships.

'What happened?' Will wondered. 'Did we kill her?'

'We broke her spell,' said Aish. 'We drove her spirit back into the deeps.'

'But how?' Will wondered. 'With one spear? And the spear so small, and the Gorm so big . . .' He was groping for logic, trying to reassure himself that he had not run mad. 'She was animated by electricity, perhaps, like a dead frog in one of Señor Galvani's experiments. And the spearhead interrupted the flow of the electrical fluid so that she could no longer hold together.'

Aish watched him, smiling fondly at his foolishness. 'It was magic, Will Dark,' she said. 'Though I confess, I am surprised it worked so well.'

They walked on side by side across the dunes. Above them the stars peeped out from their hiding places among the clouds. In Marazea the dogs were barking triumphantly, certain it was all their noise that had scared the Gorm away. Groups of people hurried about with burning torches, checking on the outlying farms. From the church huddled in the lee of the dunes, a small sound of singing voices rose.

Will and Aish picked their way down to it. When Will pushed the church door open the singing faded. There were the Dearloves and their maid, huddled around a single altar candle, terrified, but still alive.

'Is the danger passed?' asked Reverend Dearlove. 'Are we delivered from evil?'

'Will Dark has struck it down,' said Aish.

'Though I do not know how,' Will added. 'I am not sure I even hit it.'

'Come, you are too modest, Will!' said Mrs Dearlove. 'It is quite the most heroical thing I ever heard of!'

But Will did not feel like a hero. He felt that he had been of no more use than those barking dogs. He could not shake off the suspicion that the Gorm had not even felt his little spear, and had fallen apart for quite another reason of its own.

'We prayed for you, Mr Dark,' said Lucy.

Exhausted, Will lay down on the hard floor with a hassock for a pillow and slipped into a restless sleep. When he opened his eyes again, the rippled glass of the windows was starting to fill with a grey light. They went outside into the cool air and the slowly gathering dawn. The world was transformed. Weed lay everywhere, damming the streams, creating new pools and lagoons. Entangled in it were huge stones, and fish, some flapping still. The corpse of a shark hung in the pear tree. The Dearlove children moved wonderingly through the wreckage of their house, gathering up small treasures – a doll, a candlestick, a saucer from the willow-pattern tea service, miraculously unbroken. Lucy came sobbing to her mother with a shattered ornament and Mrs Dearlove put an arm around her and said, '"Lay not up for yourselves treasures upon earth, but lay up treasures in Heaven . . ."'

Aish and Will went over the dunes and down onto the beach, strolling between wrecks the Gorm had let fall there, those age-old ships, black as bog-oak, dredged from the sea-floor mud.

Reverend Dearlove came with them. In the light of day the vicar was already finding it hard to believe the things the night had shown him. 'It was only a storm, I suppose,' he kept saying. 'Just a terrible storm, a tempest or hurricane. Or perhaps it was an earthquake . . .'

'It was the Gorm,' said Will. 'You saw it, Dearlove. We both did. It stamped your house flat.'

'. . . or a waterspout, maybe,' said Dearlove. He was embarrassed by the memory of the hysterical things Will had heard him shouting in the night. 'I have read of such things happening in tropic seas. A funnel of wind sucks up the water, then sucks up sand and soil and houses as it blows ashore. Yes, that must be it; a waterspout. You can see for yourself, all this seaweed strewn about . . .'

'It was not a waterspout,' said Will, but his own memories were already growing vague, like memories of dreams; he could no longer quite recall the Gorm's shape. He wondered if the human mind was not constructed to hold such things. Or perhaps Dearlove was right, and he really had spent the night battling against nothing more than gales and landslides which his imagination had shaped into the monstrous figure of the Gorm?

Then he came around the barnacled stern of the largest wreck and looked at the sea, and the slow realization crept upon him that there was land out there. Out there

214

where no land should be, closer than any Watcher had ever seen them, and clear in the broad light of the new-risen sun, were the Hidden Lands.

He stood and stared at them until a pony came cantering along the beach with Egg on its back. 'Aish! Will Dark! Aish!' the boy was shouting. The pony was lathered with sweat. Egg reined it in and jumped down onto the sand beside it. 'Aish, I been looking for you all over. Something proper bad has happened. I don't think even you can put it right.' He sniffed loudly. Tears had drawn white paths through the dirt on his face. 'It is Utterly,' he said. 'She is gone!'

31

DOWN AMONG
THE DEAD MEN

Utterly had gone down the steep cliff paths behind the house, borne along in the lurching moonlit rush of the Men o' Weed. The one that carried her held her close against its wet chest and she kept her arms tight around its neck. At the cliff's foot the waves were breaking. So much foam was spread upon the waters beyond them, the cove looked like a heaving marble floor.

Utterly screamed as they waded into the surf with her, but it was only with the shock as ice-cold waves splashed up to soak her. She had one last glimpse of the moon, and the house far above her looking wounded and sad with the Tower gone and the roof of the study fallen in. Then the waves closed over her head and the salt sea pushed itself up her nose and down her throat. Bright bubbles were forced out of her like a mouthful of coins flung over her shoulder as a parting gift to the world she was leaving behind. The sound of the underneath of the waves rolling shoreward above her was a grumbling roar in her ears.

Utterly remembered how, long ago, she had lowered her face down into that tide-pool, and stayed for ages there breathing the same clear water as the anemones and small fish. Mr Dark said she had imagined it, and perhaps she had, but the memory was a comfort to her now. And although this water was far colder and more troubled than a tide-pool, she could breathe it just as easily. In, out, in, out . . . after a few moments it began to seem quite natural after all.

Once she was no longer worried about drowning, she was able to look about her. She saw that the deep was illumined by a faint blue light which she had not noticed in the first shock of her submersion. Perhaps it was the moon shining down through the sea's surface, or perhaps it was some deep-sea phosphorescence. She felt the Man o' Weed who held her start to change, never letting go its grip on her but losing its dense, tight-woven shape and becoming something loose and flowing, better suited to the depths. She saw that the others were shaking off their rough human forms too, unfurling into streaming things like horse-tails or long tresses of dark hair. It suited them better, she thought. They swam quite gracefully in these

217

new forms, pushing themselves with rhythmic weed-muscle pulsings of their whole selves down the long shelf of Wildsea's shore into quiet water far beneath the tumult of the waves.

Utterly had swum here before, in her dreams. She knew these swaying trunks of kelp, the shrimp and shells which clung to them, the quick nervous shoals of silvery fish that came and went in the darknesses between them. She looked down and recognized the rocks which the weeds' great holdfasts gripped like talons. She saw a ship down there, age-old, collapsing in upon itself, the sea floor round it spiky with the shards it had shed in sinking. Recalling the Gorm with its mouthful of shipwreck teeth, she thought it curious that there were any wrecks left in the deep at all, but there was another, and another . . . the hungry sea had swallowed down so many!

The weedlings wrapped their coiling fronds around her and bore her on, deeper into blue twilight and the crowding silence of the kelp.

They passed through schools of fish that were each as big as Utterly herself, and she glimpsed in the gaps between the kelp stems fish bigger still, and vast whales circling at the edges of sight. The sea grew colder, darker, deeper. The passing fish lit little lamps: pale electric freckles glowed upon their scales, and cold lanterns dangled over their toothy faces. A luminous jellyfish rippled past like a living oil lamp. From the corner of her eye Utterly glimpsed a glow shaped like a person, and she was just telling herself that she had imagined it when she saw another, and then more.

There they hung upon the cold currents, all the poor souls the sea had stolen. How they remained un-nibbled by the fish, Utterly did not know. Why they glimmered with that faint white light, she could not imagine. Perhaps they were not people really but only the shades of people, yet they turned slowly as the weedlings swam past them, as if responding to the eddyings of the water. Utterly looked into the dim lamps of their faces as she passed by.

There were hundreds of them, thousands, all around her: the drifting nation of the drowned. Some were naked, while others wore scraps of clothing which streamed out around them on the currents like the shrouds of ghosts. Some wore the uniforms of Naval men, with limpets and starfish pinned to their coats like medals. Others were in the quaint-looking clothes of bygone ages, or the shackles of slaves slung overboard upon the Middle Passage. One glittered like a merman in a coat of mail whose weight would drag him to the floor of any sea where the normal laws of nature held authority. Two fair-haired boys clung in a cold embrace. A sailor sported a tarpaulin cape which spread around him like black wings.

And still the Men o' Weed drew Utterly down and down, past this cloud-layer of the drifting dead, until below her she saw a plain as pale as a moonlit page, scrawled with the tracks of the eyeless, legless things that crept across it. She sank towards it, afraid the mud might be so soft and deep that it would swallow her. But it took her weight, and a little cloud of bubbles and pale flakes rose about her as she set down her feet.

Around her all was dark. Far above her, the drowned shone like constellations of soft stars. The Men o' Weed seemed to be of the opinion that their labours were at an end. They were losing their vigour and such shape as remained to them. Their eyes came loose and drifted two by two down to the sea floor. Their bodies became no more than stray strands of weed, animated only by the stirrings of the current.

And a voice out of the darkness said, 'Utterly!'

Utterly turned around very warily. Either her eyes were growing accustomed to the abyssal gloom or more light was growing there, for she could see things now that she had not been able to when the Men o' Weed first set her down.

A short way off, smooth buttresses of rock emerged from the ooze and sloped upwards until they were lost to sight above. At the foot of one of those buttresses stood the lady from Utterly's dreams, dressed all in white, holding out her hands in welcome.

32

THE GARDENS OF THE DEEP

'Oh, Utterly! How long I've watched you! And now here you are at last! And how *strange* you are, how small and warm, how like and not-like human beings . . . Oh, Utterly. Oh, water's daughter, welcome!'

The lady did not speak, exactly: her blue lips barely moved. But her voice found its way to Utterly's ears, carried on the water. It was the same voice Utterly had heard so often whispering to her from the waves upon the shores of Wildsea.

She walked to where the lady waited, and took the pale hand which the lady held out to her. The hand was as cold as deep water, but the lady's smile was as warm as the shallows on a summer's day. Her long hair wavered and flowed kelp-dark, veiling and unveiling the

221

whiteness of her face. Her eyes were all the colours of the sea.

They began to walk together up one of the long slopes of rock which rose from the sea bed. Walking was easy here, Utterly found, for the water helped, lifting her and propelling her gently forward each time she took a step. She felt as light as thistledown. It made her laugh. 'It is like wearing hundred-league boots,' she said. Her words sounded muffled. She imagined them echoing away from her on the tide like the long songs of whales. 'Each step here takes me ten times as far as it would on dry land!'

'The sea is better in all ways than the land,' agreed the lady. How peculiar her voice sounded, at once both far away and all around. Like the voices of distant whales must sound to men in whaleboats, setting their ears against the handles of their oars to sense the songs vibrating through the deep.

They walked on, hand in hand, through bright gardens of coral where funny little fish flitted bird-like among the deep-sea flowers. Utterly found that scents were floating on the currents, just as the smell of a bonfire was sometimes wafted across the hills to Sundown Watch. But these scents came from much further away, and as Utterly tasted each one they put pictures in her head of the places they had come from: frozen shores where icebergs calved, and isles of coral sand. And everywhere she

222

scented life: vast shoals of fish as silvery and numerous as raindrops, great whales grumbling out their songs, while in depths beyond imagining dark things for which there were no names went burrowing and groping through the slime.

'It is all yours, Utterly,' said the voice of the lady. 'Your inheritance, your playground, your own dominion.'

'But what about my friends?' said Utterly. 'I shall miss them.'

'You shall have new friends, Utterly.'

An octopus came and trailed its long arms lovingly about Utterly's neck, and a whole merry-go-round of seahorses encircled her. They distracted her for a while; the octopus was so tickly, the seahorses so sweet and comical. But then she frowned and said, 'What about Mr and Mrs Skraeveling, and Lucy Dearlove, and all the other Dearloves, and Egg, and Aish, and Uncle Will? When will I see them again?'

For the first time since Utterly met her, the lady looked displeased. 'Those names mean nothing here,' she said. 'Lives lived on land are only waves which roll and break and are forgotten. Except they are not as strong as waves, not even a little bit as strong. Mortals are no fit friends for you, Utterly. Forget them. I have brought you home.'

'This isn't my home,' said Utterly. She pulled the octopus's eight clingy legs from her neck and threw it away from her. She waved her hand, and the seahorses scattered like sparrows. She said, 'The land is my home. I live on Wildsea Island, in the Autumn Isles.'

'But there is land here too,' said the lady, recovering her smile. 'And it is far nicer than Wildsea. Come.'

They had threaded their way through the coral gardens, and now the slope that rose ahead of them was covered in fine golden sand, and lit by long fingers of light which came slanting down from somewhere overhead. Spiny urchins bustled around their feet like hedgehogs; a dogfish came nosing out of a cluster of rocks, saw them there, and fled with a quick flick of its tail. The light grew brighter, streaming down through a billowing roof of glass, and then Utterly pushed her head up through the roof and there was air beyond, and sunlight, and she was no longer weightless. Still holding her companion's hand, she waded through the surf and out onto a sandy shore.

'You see? Here is a land of your own,' said the lady. She smiled down at Utterly. Her eyes were the blue of the sunlit sea, and they shone with love and kindness. 'Don't you like it, Utterly? What troubles you?'

What troubled Utterly was the way the lady's hair continued to swirl and drift as if in water, veiling and unveiling her face. She said, 'If I may ask, if it is not a rude question . . . what is this place?'

'These are my isles. I dreamed them for myself, and now they will be yours too.'

Utterly nodded, taking this in. 'And,' she asked, 'if it is not impertinent, who are you, ma'am?'

'Why, Utterly, don't you know?'

Utterly thought she did, but she wanted to hear the lady say it. She wanted to hear it said in the voice which had whispered to her in so many dreams.

'I am the Power that dwells in the Western Deeps,' said the lady. 'I am the Gorm. I am your mother.'

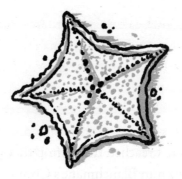

33

SHE IS NOT DROWNED

Egg told the story as he walked back up the track to
Sundown Watch, leading his pony, with Will and
Aish walking beside him. The first part of it, the attack
on the house and how Utterly had gone outside to confront
the Men o' Weed, he had been told by Mrs Skraeveling.
The sorry end he had seen with his own eyes.

When Aish and Will had gone off with his spear to
stick it in the Gorm, Egg had ridden straight to Sundown
Watch, as Aish instructed. Arriving to find the gate
locked, he had tethered the ponies to the rail outside and
clambered up the wall; it might stop sea-witches but was
no obstacle to a boy used to scrambling among the crags
of the Dizzard and bird's-nesting on the sea cliffs at Stack.
From the wall's top he had looked into the gardens, and

there he had seen the crowd of weed-men carrying Utterly away around the side of the house.

'So I jumped down into the garden,' he said. 'I think I squashed some kind of bush, I'm sorry about that. And I followed them round the house and down across the grass to where the cliff starts, but they was faster than me. By the time I reached the clifftop they was already at its bottom, down in Blanchmane's Cove.'

'And what of Utterly?' asked Will.

Egg sniffed sharply. He did not want anyone to see him cry, but he had been crying on and off ever since it happened. It had been so wrong, felt so unfair, after all the efforts he and Aish had made to bring about a happy ending. It made Egg feel the way he had when a cow had kicked him in the goolies once: sort of stunned and not believing it at first, and then this unmanly urge to blub. He wiped the heel of one grimy hand across his face and said, 'They took her, didn't they? They waded out into the waves, and they took Utterly with them, down into the sea. They drowned her, Aish. They drowned her.'

'So it was not our spear that made the Gorm collapse at all,' said Will, when they had walked on in silence for a while. Through the numbness of his grief for Utterly he felt a faint sense of relief. He had never really believed he was a giant-slayer. 'The Gorm had simply finished the job she came to do,' he said. 'She outgeneralled us, and while we were distracted by her tantrums she sent her

227

weed-men sneaking round behind us. As soon as they had Utterly in their clutches, there was no more need for giants, nor for tantrums. Utterly was what she came for.'

'I should have guarded the girl closer,' said Aish, wiping tears away. She had taken off her antlers and carried them in her hand, as if she thought antlers too proud for this sad morning. 'I should have guessed the Gorm would want her. Utterly is what it has all been about. I knew the day I first lit eyes on her she belonged partly to the sea. I thought that charm I gave her might have anchored her to the land, but my magic was not strong enough . . .'

They reached the gate, went through it, and there was Mrs Skraeveling waiting, calling from the open doorway, 'Oh, Master Will, Master Will . . .'

Will stopped as they went up the path, stooped and picked up something that had been half trodden into the mossy turf between the paving stones. It was the green stone pendant. He gave it to Aish. 'The string has not been broken,' he said. 'It is as though she took it off willingly . . .'

'Oh, Master Will,' sniffled Mrs Skraeveling. 'You have heard the dreadful news?'

'Egg told us everything,' said Will. 'Are you and Mr Skraeveling unhurt?'

'Those villains offered me no violence, sir,' said Mrs Skraeveling, 'but Skraeveling took such a blow upon his head when they threw him into the wall, and I think his arm is broke. I have sent him to his bed and told him to stay there until the doctor can be called over from Merriport. But, oh, sir, they took our Utterly! Our little kitten! How could they do such wickedness? She went out to meet them so bravely, thinking she might save me and Skraeveling from more peril, and they took her, sir, they took her and drowned her in the cold sea.'

'She is not drowned,' said Will.

He said it with such certainty that the others all stared at him as if they feared he had gone mad.

'But I saw 'em at it, Mr Dark,' said Egg very gently. 'I wish it was not so, but 'twas. I saw 'em wade into the sea with her, and go under it, and I waited on the shore an age and watched, but they never came up again.'

Mrs Skraeveling patted Will's arm. 'Why don't you come on inside, Master Will. We shall find you a glass of brandy, and take a look at that bump upon your head . . .'

'I am not wandering in my wits, Mrs S,' said Will. 'I am thinking clearly, for the first time since I returned to this curious island of ours. Aish is right. Utterly *does* have something of the sea about her. She came from the sea! Did you know she hatched out from a mermaid's purse? She was the Gorm's gift to my brother. Now the Gorm has taken her back, and would surely not have gone to such trouble simply to drown her? No, Utterly will be quite all right beneath the sea. *Water is as good as air to them as dwell under the Gorm's enchantments.*'

'But if she ain't drowned,' said Egg, 'where is she?'

'Why, where do you think?' said Will, laughing at being posed such a simple question. He pointed west, where the Hidden Lands sat on the sea looking as clear and as solid as if they had been there always. 'Those islands are the Gorm's home, are they not? They are the source of all the strangeness that washes around Wildsea's shores. That is where I will find Utterly.'

'But you cannot mean to go there!' said Aish. For the first time in their acquaintance Will saw her look afraid. 'Not across the sea!'

'You ain't got a boat,' Egg pointed out.

'Thurza Froy has a boat,' said Will. 'And since I presume she is buried beneath the rubble of St Chyan's Head, she will not be needing it any further. I will want provisions for the journey. Perhaps Mr Skraeveling will lend me his pistol . . .'

He had felt so weary walking up the track, thinking Utterly dead and drowned. Now hope had woken him; he did not feel at all like a man who had been up fighting weed-giants all night, but like an explorer preparing a great adventure. Utterly was on the islands; she had to be. He ran into the house. Egg and the women followed him as he went from room to room, gathering things he thought he would need.

'Do you know how to sail a boat, Master Will?'

'I went out in one with my friend Constantine, on

Derwentwater, in the North-country,' said Will. 'I did not control the vessel myself, but I think I recall how it was steered, what strings are pulled to raise the sail, et cetera.'

'You cannot go alone, Will Dark,' said Aish.

But Will knew he could not ask anyone else to go with him. It was a dangerous voyage he proposed, and probably a watery grave at the end of it. He did not fear it, because to die trying to rescue Utterly would be better than to live knowing he had failed her. But he could not allow anyone else to endanger themselves for him. He had endangered them all enough with his fire, and besides, what help could they be against the power of the Gorm? The only person who might help him was Aish herself, and he could see from the look on her face that she was too afraid of the sea to offer.

He said gently, 'It is my duty to go, Aish, and no one else's. But I should be exceeding grateful were you to come with me as far as the Undercliff, to help me get safely aboard the witch's boat.'

'I shall, Will Dark,' said Aish unhappily. 'But there will be nothing *safe* about it. Whoever heard of anyone ever being safe aboard a boat?'

34

SETTING SAIL

In the end, it was quite a procession that went down onto the Undercliff that morning. Neither Egg nor Mrs Skraeveling would think of staying behind, and when Mr Skraeveling heard that Will was disobeying his wife's advice he said there was no reason why he shouldn't too, and climbed out of his bed to join the party with his arm in a sling and a crown of bandages around his battered head.

As they passed the ruins of the vicarage, Mrs Dearlove and her children came running to tell them the news from Marazea. 'No one was killed, nor even badly hurt, though several houses were knocked down. Some cattle have run away, and some sheep are dead, but sheep are always dying. Reverend Dearlove has gone to give what help he may, while the rest of us remained behind to try and – well . . .' Mrs Dearlove's voice trailed off. She gestured at the mound of rubble which had been her home.

'We shall rebuild it,' Will promised. 'The other houses too; bigger and better than before. And until that can be done, you must move into Sundown Watch. There is plenty of room, and Utterly will be glad of friends her own age about the place when I bring her home.'

'Bring her home?' asked Mrs Dearlove, looking uncertainly at him, and then at the rest of his party. When Will's plan was explained to her she shook her head doubtfully, but she and her children joined the expedition to the Undercliff too, trailing behind Will as if he was already dead and they were his mourners.

As they followed the coast path northward they were hailed by some bold young fellows who had come over from Stack to see the devastation. Will did not want to stop and look at whatever it was the men had found, but their shouts were so urgent that he turned aside and went down onto the beach where they were gathered. His followers crowded behind as he stood and looked down at the two dead bodies lying on the sand.

'Washed ashore on the tide, Watcher.'

''Tis the very same place they found your brother, God rest him.'

Thurza Froy looked like a draggled waxwork of herself,

wrapped in a tattered shroud of weed and half-buried in the sand. Beside her lay a form so horrible that Mrs Dearlove shrieked when she saw it, and Lucy declared she was sure it would haunt her nightmares.

'We thought it was a great dead fish at first,' said one of the men. 'Do you know what manner o' thing it be, Mr Dark?'

Will did. He had seen pictures of diving suits, although never one as primitive as this. Its glass eyes stared skyward as coldly as the dead eyes of a shark, and water seeped from all its seams and sutures. 'It is Davey Froy,' he said. 'He is wearing the diving suit that Thurza made for him.'

'It can't be, sir – 'tis forty year or more since Davey Froy was lost.'

'Thurza believed he was waiting for her in the Hidden Lands,' said Will. He stooped and found the rusty latches which held the suit's hood in place. He did not know what he expected to see when he pulled the hood off – Davey Froy's bones, or Davey Froy himself, looking as young and handsome as the day he'd drowned. But when he got the latches open and dragged it free, a rush of salt water spilled out of the neck of the suit, and it subsided slowly like a punctured balloon. There had been nothing inside it but the sea.

❖

If Will's friends had been hoping that finding the drowned sea-witch would distract him from his plans, they were disappointed; he was soon hurrying on his way again, muttering about getting afloat before the tide turned.

If they hoped that the Gorm had stamped on Thurza's boat, or the storm had washed it away, they were disappointed all over again when they reached the Undercliff. The witch's hovel had been flattened by a landslip, but the boat was whole, hidden under its tarpaulins on the beach below.

The men from Stack had come along. They turned the boat upright and rolled it down the beach on some logs Thurza had kept there for the purpose. They stepped the mast and set the rudder on its pintles. They rigged the sail and gave Will brief lessons in its raising and lowering. When the boat was in the water with the small waves breaking around it and starting to lift it, Egg waded in to help them steady it, and even Mrs Dearlove kicked off her shoes, pulled off her stockings, hitched up her skirts, and went in up to her knees.

But Aish, though she was barefoot already, could not bring herself to let her toes touch the waves, or even the wet shingle at the water's edge. She stood safely out of the sea's reach, looking miserable. When Will came awkwardly to say goodbye she took out the green stone pendant he had given back to her and hung it around his neck, tucking the stone inside his shirt. 'I am glad I found you on the beach, Will Dark,' she said. 'You are the best thing the sea ever washed up.'

'I'm not,' said Will. 'Utterly is.'

He said his goodbyes to the others, and patted his coat pockets to check that he still had Mr Skraeveling's gun and a canvas bag containing the powder, shot and wadding he would need to reload it. Mrs Skraeveling passed him a packet of sandwiches she had made, and he climbed into the boat. The Stack men gave it a push to set it going, and he gripped the tiller as it coasted out between the sharp black rocks which lay just offshore. He was trying not to recall his last sea voyage, and how that had turned out.

On the shingle, Mrs Dearlove led her children in a prayer. Egg did not join in. What good was praying likely to do? He knew the Dearloves' God had no authority over the deeps, for all they liked to carry on about those who went down to the sea in ships and had business in great waters.

'We should've gone with him, Aish,' he said sulkily, crossing the tideline to stand beside her. 'You rescued him out of the sea, are you goin' to just let the sea take him again? And what about Utterly? I don't reckon he can get her back without help. It ain't right letting him go off alone. He ain't got no more sense than a baby.' He felt ready to cry again, and was hiding it as best he could by growing angry.

He waited for Aish to change her mind, to call the boat back and climb aboard. But Aish just stood there, watching it depart, and weeping quietly with pity, or perhaps with shame.

'Well, *someone* has to go with him,' said Egg indignantly. He looked round at the others, realized that the only someone available was him, and said it again to try and convince himself. '*Someone* has to go.' The gap that separated the witch's boat from the shore was widening. Before it could grow too wide or his fear of the water too great, Egg went sprinting down the beach and threw himself into the waves.

'Egg!' shouted Aish, and the others all joined in with her. 'Egg! Egg! Come back, Egg!'

Egg ignored them all. He waded into the sea till he could wade no more, then started swimming. It was a lot like swimming in the Dizzard's little lakes, except the sea was more of a bully than any lake. It kept lifting him up and trying to shove him back towards the shore, where Aish was leaning out as far as she dared over the water to reach for him. Mrs Dearlove had waded in again. Egg butted his head into the waves, kicking and flailing, spluttering in shock when salt water went up his nose. Then, just as even he was starting to think he had made a mistake, the planks of the witch's boat were suddenly in front of him, and Will was reaching over the side to grab him by his hair, his arms, and heave him on board.

'You foolish boy! What are you playing at?'

Egg knelt gasping on a thwart while Will tried to turn back to shore. But the offshore breeze had found the boat by then; when Will put the rudder over, the sail flapped violently and the boom swung across, almost knocking Egg back overboard. People on the shore yelled advice which Will could not hear, and which he doubted he would have understood if he had.

'You can't take me back to the beach,' said Egg. 'Not with the wind against you and all them vicious rocks. Not unless you want us to be wrecked before we even start.'

There did seem to be truth in that. Will let the prow swing towards the Hidden Lands again, the wind leaned comfortably on the sail, and the water began to chuckle along the boat's sides as it glided smoothly out from the shadow of the cliffs and into sunshine.

'Then I am afraid you will have to come with me,' said Will. He tried to make light of the prospect. 'It will be a proper expedition now there are two of us. Like Captain Cook setting forth for the Antipodes . . .'

But Egg had never heard of Captain Cook, and he was already regretting his bravery. He shaded his eyes against the morning sun and looked back to shore. Aish was running along the beach, waving, and probably shouting his name. But Egg was already so far from land he could not hear her, and in a minute more all he could see of her was the russety splodge of her dress, and the lighter-coloured splodges which were Mrs Dearlove and the other women, running to comfort Aish as she fell to her knees upon the shingle.

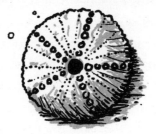

35

THE TOWER IN THE WEST

Utterly walked with the lady on the shore. The cliffs behind the golden beach were a fairyland of sea-carved arches, tide-pools, little waterfalls and shady, dripping caves. The lady knelt and picked some of the small pink daisies that grew in the grass at the top of the beach, where the cliffs began. She plaited them with great care into a little bracelet. She said, 'I made you one like this when you were tiny, Utterly. Do you have it still?'

Utterly shook her head.

The lady sighed. Her eyes, which had been so blue, seemed more green or turquoise now, the sweet melancholy colours of the sea at evening. 'I left it on the shore for you,' she said. 'I hoped your father would let you keep it, so you would know where you came from.'

All her life Utterly had dreamed of having a mother. She had always felt envious of more fortunate children like the Dearloves, whose mothers were still alive. She had always imagined that if, by some miracle, she ever met *her* mother, she would know her at once, and love her completely. But now the miracle had occurred, she did not know what she felt. She had never imagined a mother who was quite so strange as this, or quite so powerful, or quite so inclined to shift from one form to another, taking on the guise of frightening weed-men, or gigantic monsters. It seemed very curious that this pretty lady who smiled so fondly at her was also the towering, flailing, howling thing she had seen rising from the sea last night. When she had imagined having a mother she had imagined someone who would play with her, and teach her to be ladylike, and sit by her bed all night if she was sick. It was hard to imagine the Gorm doing any of those things.

On the other hand, it did make her feel rather important, being the child of the Gorm. It made her understand herself. This was why the sea had talked to her, and why she had never been afraid of it.

Utterly held out her hand and let the lady tie the bracelet round her wrist.

It was then that she realized the cliffs which rose over her were not cliffs at all. A palace stood there on the shore. It was dark and sea-stained at the base, which must be why Utterly had thought it only outcroppings of rock, but

241

it rose to tall white turrets, arching buttresses, gleaming roofs of gold and silver. Windows glittered in the sunlight high above, and low down, not far from where Utterly and the lady stood, there was a narrow doorway shaped rather like a keyhole.

The lady let go Utterly's hand and walked to the doorway. She turned there, framed against the darkness within, beckoning. Utterly followed her inside. Stone stairs led upward in a spiral. Utterly's footsteps echoed on them. The feet of the lady who went ahead of her made no sound at all, but the edges of her skirts whispered as they brushed against the walls on either side.

The climb reminded Utterly of something, but she was not sure what it was until she reached the top and scrambled up into the blur of sea light from six big windows. The walls were of bone-pale stone, the windows open to the air, but the whole place was an echo or reflection of the Tower at Sundown Watch. When she looked from the eastern window, Utterly saw, far off, a low blue island with three mountains on it, rising from the sea's rim, and a bright star shining on its shore which she knew must be the afternoon sun gleaming on the windows of her home.

Below the window, where the Watcher's desk should stand, was a stone table on which a book lay open. The pages were covered with lines of writing in grey ink. When Utterly tried to read what was written there it made no

242

sense at first, as if it was not really writing but just the sort of mindless patterns worms made sometimes on the surface of driftwood. Then, as if whoever had made the marks had been slowly working out how to form them, she began to discern the shapes of letters . . .

i i i de e p

. . . and then the letters started to form words . . .

deep in the cold in the blue cold dark in the long wash the tide in the dark in the deep dark i watch i watch i hunger deep i wait i watch in the deep

. . . and then the words began to make sense.

i watch i watch I watch I see him walking on the shore I watch him as he watches me and writes small thoughts in his big book there were others before this one but this one interests me how does he live knowing that he is mortal and will die how do any of them live on land knowing that all land is mortal and my sea will devour it in the end how does he not despair?

I took a form that would not frighten him and stepped out of the sea to speak with him. His name is andrewedark and he had no answers to my questions but I love him poor mortal land-thing I love him because I pity him because he is so fragile and will never know the beauties of the deeps.

243

Utterly glanced over her shoulder. The lady stood behind her, watching her read. It seemed odd that the Gorm should have kept her own Log. How had something like the Gorm even learned to write? Then Utterly recalled the strewn weed in Blanchmane's Cove and how it had looked almost like a message scrawled there. Perhaps there was nothing the Gorm could not do if she put her vast watery mind to the task. Perhaps keeping this Log had been part of her way of seeking to understand Mr Dark. She had not been very good at it though, thought Utterly. Her grammar and punctuation were shocking. Also, none of the entries was dated, and in the gaps between them, months or years seemed to elapse.

I did not expect a child to come, the Gorm had written. *The idea of andrewedark fell into my mind like a seed and took root and grew into a baby. I took on the form of a great she-shark and birthed it in a lovely egg and then I became a wave and carried it to wildsea for andrewedark to find upon the shore it is a baby of his kind not mine and he will know what to do with it and there is an end of it.*

The name that he has given her is UTTERLY I do not know why.

I cannot keep from watching her. Utterly. She is small and odd and ugly but she is mine. She is growing and the more she grows

244

the more I long for her I went onto the shore when andrewedark was walking on the beach with her but he took her away before she saw me.

He makes sure she stays away from the sea now where I cannot walk in any form that would not scare her so I weave bodies of weed and creep onto the land in them and watch her secretly through their eyes so soft she is so fragile so beloved so Utterly.

Sometimes I grow so distracted watching her that I let my weed-body dry out and then I cannot stay in it and leave it lying there a tangle of kelp stranded far from the tideline as a puzzle to amuse the mortals.

It is intolerable that my child should live on land I want her back.

I spoke with andrewedark on the beach. It is many years since I saw him he is older now they age so fast. As Utterly must age if she remains with him.

Give her back to me I told him but he defied me – me who was old already when the first fish swam! Let her stay he said I love her too he said take me instead he said.

The fool is dead. He threw himself into the waves as if he

thought it was only a drowned body I wanted as if I do not al-
ready have more than enough of those I did not want his corpse
I let him wash ashore but out of pity for him I shall let Utterly
stay on land.

I watch her still.

I watch her still. I call out to her to let her know of my
longing and sometimes she almost wakes and almost hears.
She watches me now as he once did. She has spoken with
the old Sea-witch and with the one who lives in the woods.
It is time for her to learn of her true nature. Soon I shall gather
her up and she will leave the land behind and learn to love
the sea.

The writing ended, or seemed to trail off, the last
words very faint. It seemed a pity, when the Gorm had
just been learning how to use full stops. So I had a
father and a mother, Utterly thought, and she felt very
sorry that Mr Dark had not chosen to tell her the truth
about herself. A great many things occurred to her that
she would have liked to tell him too, but now she would
never have the chance.

Then she looked at the book again and saw that more
letters were appearing there, oozing slowly out of nowhere
onto the page. It was as if worms really were writing them,
but the worms were invisible, and the greyish letters were
being squeezed out of them reluctantly.

They called to me with fire from the heights. The Sea-witch
set her knife against Utterly's neck. I was so angry I have not
been so angry in a thousand years I

Utterly watched, waiting for the Gorm's account
of its last night's rampage, and perhaps to read of her
own journey into the deep and her arrival here upon
the Hidden Lands. But the writing had stopped again.
She looked round at the lady, but the lady's eyes were no
longer on her. They had turned an ominous grey, and
were staring over Utterly's head, out across the sea.

Utterly turned to see what had displeased her mother.
Far out beyond the offshore reefs a sail showed, golden
with the light of the westering sun, like a single small
flame burning on the water. The lady watched it, and her
eyes grew colder, and greyer, and the sound of the waves
on the shore became harsher.

'Who is it?' asked Utterly. 'Do you think it is Uncle
Will?' She remembered how he had come to find her
when she ran away to talk to Aish, and found she felt the
same way now that she had then – ashamed of herself
for putting him to the trouble of following her, but very
pleased that he had taken it. Then she grew afraid for
him, for this was not the Dizzard, and this lady was not
Aish, and she was not likely to welcome him – it seemed
more probable she would grow angry again and cause a
great wave to overwhelm the little boat.

'Oh, please let him come ashore safe!' she begged.

The lady seemed amused at that, but underneath her look of laughter there was something sterner, older, colder. 'Forget him, Utterly,' she said. 'Those mortals you were raised among are nothing to you now.'

Utterly felt confused. What a thing to ask of her. How could she possibly obey? 'I can't forget Uncle Will!' she said. 'That would be like forgetting Mr and Mrs Skraeveling, or Lucy and Horatio, or Mrs Dearlove, or the vicar, or Aish, or Egg, or—'

'Forget them,' said the lady, and her voice was suddenly loud, like the breaking of a seventh wave, which anyone sea-wise knew was bigger and stronger than the six before. The sound rolled right through Utterly's head, and when it went sighing back the sandcastle of her memories had been washed away. Only a few blurred relics remained, glimpses of faces she could almost put a name to, and people who seemed now like people only met in dreams.

She looked at the window, but the boat had passed out of view, and she could no longer recall the name of that far-off island across the sea. She looked down at the book on the stone table, but it was not a book at all, and she was not sure now that it ever had been: it was only an old driftwood log, on which sea-worms had left wandering trails which looked almost like writing.

36

A VOYAGE OF EXPLORATION

Will was secretly glad that Egg had decided to join the expedition. It was useful to have another pair of eyes aboard to keep a lookout for rocks and other perils while his were distracted by the view ahead. His family had spent so long watching for those improbable islands, and now he was the first to see them clear, and he could not keep his attention from straying to them. He was afraid that if he glanced away they might hide themselves again, and take Utterly with them.

For a time the islands seemed to be drawing no closer, as if they were travelling into the west at the same speed as the boat. But gradually it became possible to make out details which had eluded all the previous Watchers. It was clear that there were three islands, separated from each other by narrow straits, each with its own mountain. The nearest appeared to be the largest. Soon Will could see the waves breaking on its beaches and white waterfalls plunging down its cliffs.

'An entire new land mass,' he said. 'I suppose it will need a name. What do you reckon, Egg? Dark's Isle? Utterly Island? And Egg Harbour for our landing site, perhaps . . .'

'Gormsland,' said Egg, and wished he hadn't, because it made him think of all the cold fathoms of empty water swirling and shifting under him, and what horrors might be lurking there.

As if to prove his fears well-founded, a sea dragon suddenly lifted its head out of the waves not twenty feet from him. It glanced disapprovingly at the boat and snorted a plume of spray out of a blowhole between its eyes. The spray drifted downwind to spatter the sail and Egg's face. Will, terribly alarmed, pulled out Mr Skraeveling's pistol, cocked it and fired.

'Don't!' shouted Egg. 'Aish says there ain't no harm in sea dragons. Not 'less you happen to be a fish, she says.'

Will was already regretting his shot. The ancient pistol had not been built for accuracy, and the movement of the boat had spoiled his aim. He had probably endangered himself more than the dragon, for scraps of burning wadding were blowing back into the boat, and he and Egg almost overturned it in their efforts to stamp them out before they started a fire.

The dragon did not seem interested in the passing boat at all. Now Will saw that there were others of its breed nearby, their black bodies and black swan necks rising and turning playfully among the waves. A half-dozen of the creatures had hauled themselves out of the water entirely and lay sunning themselves upon a sloping shelf of rock. After a few moments the one which had snorted dipped its head beneath the surface again. Egg leaned over the rail and watched it pass beneath the keel with a few powerful strokes of its paddle-shaped limbs. It swam off quickly towards the north.

'Extraordinary brute,' muttered Will, putting away the pistol and moving the tiller to steer the boat well clear of the dragon's bathing-spot. 'One of my ancestors claimed the Hidden Lands were the home of creatures which do not belong in our ordinary world. He said they were the source of all our tales of sea serpents . . .'

Before they could debate this possibility, something that turned out to be only a rock came scraping its way along the keel, and the boat was suddenly among reefs. There was a period of confusion, Will shouting orders, the sail fluttering as Egg clumsily lowered it. Then, somehow, they were in calm water, and small waves were carrying them in to ground on a beach beneath tall black cliffs.

Will climbed over the bows and dropped into the shallows. He still half expected even then to find the island was an illusion, but its wet sand was as firm and real as the sand that edged Wildsea. He had been hoping Utterly would have seen the boat coming and be waiting at the landing place, but the beach was empty. At one end a waterfall splattered down the rocks and carved a passage through the sand. At the other, the cliffs rose in a confusion of arches and pillars and domes so huge and so fantastical that it took Will and Egg a while to understand they were not cliffs at all, but buildings.

'And how did we not notice them when we were sailing in?' asked Egg.

'The dragons distracted us,' said Will. 'And the light was in our eyes. It is the Mansions of the Gorm, just as Thurza Froy reported them, except they are above the sea today and not beneath it.' Though now he came to study the buildings, there was something submarine about the way the sunlight rippled and danced across them, and about the flocks of little birds which flickered songlessly about their fish-scale roofs. If you looked at them too long, he thought, you might find yourself thinking that they were really deep beneath the waves . . .

They dragged the boat well up the beach. They cupped their hands around their mouths and shouted, 'Utterly!' Echoes came back at them from the cliffs. Will reloaded Mr Skraeveling's pistol, and started along the beach towards the buildings. Egg hung back, and when Will looked round he caught a look of fear on the boy's face before Egg hid it under his idea of a manly scowl.

252

'You should stay here and watch the boat, perhaps,' Will suggested gently.

'Not likely!' said Egg. 'I'm sticking with you, Watcher.'

'And I am glad of it,' said Will. It was true; he would hate to be alone in this eerie place. Yet he was not happy to think that he was leading the boy into more danger. He stood uncertainly for a moment, wondering what to do, and suddenly remembered the holed stone which hung around his neck. He took it off and handed it to Egg. 'Aish gave me this,' he said. 'I'm sure she would rather you had it.'

'I don't know if Aish's magic works in a place like this,' said Egg. 'I reckon that's why she couldn't come herself.' But he took the charm, and slipped the string over his head, and was glad of the small, solid weight of Wildsea stone against his chest as he followed Will into the Mansions of the Gorm.

37

THE STATUES

Utterly's mother, like so many grown-ups, seemed uncertain how to speak to children. She kept her silence for the most part as she led Utterly through the pillared halls and passageways of her mansion. Sometimes she would pause beside a chest or alcove and fetch out another present for her daughter – a gown of green silk; three jewelled rings. The gown was the prettiest thing Utterly had ever worn, and the rings so pleasantly heavy on her fingers that she felt sure they must be worth kings' ransoms, but her favourite was still the little bracelet of pink daisies: it was not so precious, but it was more precious to her.

'Utterly!' called distant voices, just as the waves had called to her, on another island, long ago. But these were not the voices of the waves. When the lady heard them her eyes turned suddenly pale, like the surface of the sea when a squall approaches.

'Utterly!' came the voices, echoing.

Utterly wondered who they were, and what they wanted with her.

❖

Dwarfed by huge pillars and towering doorways, cowed to silence by the silences in empty colonnades, Will and Egg wandered through the Mansions of the Gorm like travellers among the ruins of the Pharaohs, except that they paused every few yards to shout, 'Utterly?'

There was never any reply: only the echoes, flitting ahead of them. They followed, down a long curve of marble stairs, in through an archway that gaped like the mouth of Jonah's whale. It opened onto a circular, pillared hall so large that it reminded Will of the Rotunda at Ranelagh pleasure gardens, and Egg of a big clearing in the woods. Its floor was tiled in shimmering gold. Its high roof was a dome of glass through which the evening sunlight came dancing down. The room was so deep that the sunlight did not reach all the way down into it, but from the pillars which surrounded it hung beautiful lamps, casting their soft light over a silent crowd of women.

Egg and Will stood frozen in the doorway, feeling like interlopers at a ball, until they realized that the women were not real, but only statues.

They went forward slowly, watched by stony eyes in stony faces, and by eyes of ivory and lapis lazuli in bronze ones. The statues were of all sorts and sizes. A head as big as a small house lay in the shadows; figurines no longer than Egg's forefinger littered the floor. Most were human-sized, and most were beautiful. Even the oldest – squat bulbous things with gaping mouths and holes for eyes – were probably some shaggy sculptor's long-ago idea of beauty.

'Who are they all?' Egg asked, in the hushed whisper that the place seemed to demand.

'They are her,' said Will. 'Thalassa. Tethys. Tiamat. The Gorm. Sedna. T'ien Fei. They are all statues of her, or people's notion of her. She is vain. She has collected idols of herself from sunken temples, foundered ships . . .'

'They make her look prettier than she did last night,' said Egg, disturbed by all those unblinking eyes.

'She can take many forms, Egg,' said Will. He moved between the statues. Some had been so long beneath the waves that their lovely faces were acned with barnacles. Some had been the stem-posts or figureheads of ancient ships; they met his gaze with painted eyes.

'Which is the real Gorm then?' asked Egg. 'What is she really?'

'I think she is what people used to call a goddess,' said Will. 'But really I think she is more like . . . the *idea* of the sea, come to life. I think in long ago times every island had a goddess of its own. Some still do, I believe. But the Gorm was more powerful than any of them, for their domains were bounded by their islands' shores, while the whole watery world was hers to rule. As for human beings, we were only her playthings. But we grew strong, and nowadays most of us do not even believe in her, and so she has come to live mostly apart from us, in this shadow-place that comes and goes as if even she does not believe in it entirely. I expect she misses being worshipped. Perhaps that is why she has assembled this collection.'

The room darkened. Will looked up. Above the high glass roof the sky was turning to the deep blue of evening. Late sunlight rippled across the walls up there. From somewhere outside came the sound of the sea beating steadily against the shore.

'The tide has turned,' said Egg.

Something moved among the crowding statues. A flake of colour darting like a hummingbird. It had emerged, Will thought, from between the slightly parted lips of that huge stone head. It hid for a moment behind another of the statues, then flitted out to hover a few inches from his face.

It was a fish. It hung in the air, flicking a fin now and then, its mouth opening and closing, its golden eyes regarding Will with such a meaningful expression that he wondered if the Gorm herself was looking out through them.

This was the Gorm's world, Will knew that. If islands could come and go upon her whim, then why should a fish not fly? The normal rules were all suspended here. But he had lived all of his twenty-two years in another world, and everything he had learned there told him that where a fish could live and breathe, Will Dark could not.

The sound of the waves had grown louder, and they were speaking to him.

'*You are deep under water,*' they told him.

He looked up again, and saw at once that the elegant glass roof was not a roof at all. It was the surface of the sea, seen from beneath. The pillars that supported it were only buttresses of rock, the whole wide chamber just a deep cavern among sea cliffs. *Water is as good as air to them as dwell under the Gorm's enchantments*, Thurza Froy had said, but it seemed in this case air *was* water. Will felt the weight of it pressing down on him. It soaked coldly through his clothes. He turned to call out a warning to Egg, and bubbles blurted from his mouth.

'What is it now?' asked Egg, watching the Watcher gag and gurn at him. He had not seen the fish. He did not see the bubbles either. There were no words he could hear in the sound of the waves. The air was still air to him, the room a room.

But panic had taken hold of Will. The memories of his shipwreck crashed down on him and made him fear that he was still in the water off Three Sisters Reef, and everything that had happened since the *Boldventure* ran aground had been just the dreams of a drowning man. He struggled to swim towards the light and air so far above, but the pistol in his coat weighted him to the floor as if his pockets had been filled with stones. Egg watched him shrug the coat off, and remarked that it fell very slowly, drifting to the floor where flakes of gold rose glittering around it as it settled. But he did not wonder why, for he was too busy watching Will kick and flail himself free of the ground and rise clumsily upward, not flying so much as swimming on the air, up and up till he was just a struggling frog-shape against the evening sky.

'Will Dark?' Egg shouted after him. 'Where are you going to?'

Far above him, Will smashed through the ceiling. Egg hid his face for fear of falling glass, but none came down on him. When he looked up again, Will was lost to sight.

'Flown off like a bird,' muttered Egg. 'And left me all alone.' He spoke aloud, thinking it would help him to keep his nerve, but it had the opposite effect – his voice sounded small and lonely in the silence of the big room. The statues seemed to be listening.

Egg put his hand to his chest, and touched the holed stone that hung there. It felt warm and dry. It reminded him of the good dark soil of the Dizzard, and Aish's voice as she went singing through the woods. Aish would not be afraid of a gaggle of old statues, he told himself, so why should he? He glowered at them, trying to stare them down.

It was then he realized, with a shock that went through him like a thunderbolt, that not all of them were statues.

On the far side of the chamber a lady in a white dress stood watching him. Egg could not be sure at what point in the proceedings she had arrived, but he was certain she had not been there a minute ago. She was as pale as marble and as still as stone, but he saw her eyes move, and the black cloud of her hair swirl stormily around her face. One of her long white hands lay on the shoulder of a girl who stood beside her, and the girl was no statue either. The girl wore a gown of green silk, and her fingers glittered with rings, and a slender crown studded with bright jewels was on her brow. It took Egg a moment to recognize Utterly under all that finery, and when he looked into her eyes he saw that she did not recognize him either. Which made no sense to Egg, because *he* was not wearing fancy dress.

'Utterly,' he said, trying to ignore the sea-cold stare of the lady who stood beside her. 'I've come to fetch you home.'

38

UTTERLY UNBOUND

Utterly could not imagine how he knew her name. Who was he, this impertinent boy? He looked so out of place here in her mother's realm, and he stood so stiffly, his fists clenched, his feet planted wide apart, his chin raised, ready for a fight he could not win.

'There's a boat waiting, Utterly,' he said. 'And your uncle Will is here somewhere.'

He is called Egg, thought Utterly. But she was not sure where that thought had come from, and she felt certain it must be wrong. What sort of a name was Egg?

The lady let her hand slip from Utterly's shoulder. She walked slowly towards Egg while her eyes took on the grey of Arctic seas and her hair coiled above her head like a black snake readying itself to strike.

261

Unsettled by her steady gaze, Egg tried making conversation. 'I been looking at your statues,' he said. 'They ain't much like you.'

The lady smiled. It was not the gentle smile some of her statues wore. The people who carved those had been trying to make the old Gorm out to be nicer than she was, Egg reckoned. This smile she smiled at him was cold and mocking, and her lips were a cheerless blue. 'I have worn many faces,' she said, in a voice that was mostly echoes, coming from all around him. 'Am I not beautiful?'

Egg shrugged.

'You should have gone with your master,' the lady said. 'I chose to show you mercy, for the sake of Utterly. But you have stayed. You should leave now, before I drown you.'

Egg thought longingly of the boat waiting on the beach. His feet itched to run, but he stood his ground. 'I'll go all right,' he said. 'But Utterly is coming home with me.'

The lady opened her mouth surprisingly wide and made a terrifying sound. She bellowed like a storm-wind whistling across the whole wide Atlantic to slam waves against the rocks of Wildsea. For the first time, Egg truly believed she was the same thing he had watched rampaging in the night.

'*Utterly must stay!*' she howled.

Egg put his head down and leaned stubbornly into the

gale of her wrath. 'Who says so?' he asked indignantly. 'That's up to Utterly, ain't it? Why not let her decide?' He looked at Utterly. She still stood where the lady had left her, blinking at him like a sleepwalker. 'Don't you want to come home to Wildsea with me, Utterly?'

Utterly struggled to remember what that word meant. Wildsea. It made her think of a window with the evening sea outside it.

'But this is my home,' she said. 'This lady is my mother.'

'Funny sort of mother,' said Egg. 'She sealed you up inside a mermaid's purse and threw you to Andrewe Dark like loose change.' He shrugged like a boy who knew a bit about the world, and said, 'Just 'cos she's your mum don't mean you have to stay here with her, not if you don't want to. I didn't stay with my dad, because he was an old bully, and cruel. Aish and the Dizzard people have been better family to me than *he* ever was. And it looks to me like this mother of yours is a cruel old bully too. She's got a temper on her all right – I saw her last night, as tall as the sky, howling and carrying on and stamping folk's shippens flat. She may give you pretty frocks and diamonds and things, but that don't mean much. I reckon your uncle Will and Mr and Mrs Skraeveling up at Sundown Watch are better family to you than she'll ever be.'

Uncle Will, the Skraevelings, Sundown Watch . . . The names he spoke lit pictures in Utterly's head as bright and vivid as magic lantern slides. Far away it felt, and long ago, but she could see it clearly, that former life of hers. There was the house called Sundown Watch, where for a little while she had been the Watcher. There was her bedroom, and there was the little carved tortoise on the landing newel post. There was Mrs Skraeveling making pastry in the kitchen with her sleeves rolled up and a smudge of flour on her red face, and Mr Skraeveling busy with the garden. It felt to Utterly as if she had liked that life very much.

She would be very sad if it were gone for ever.

Egg kept his eyes on Utterly, pleased with her for waking from whatever enchantment she had been under, and pleased with himself for having woken her. He did not notice the lady moving closer. He did not see his danger till she darted out her hand and snatched the stone that hung around his neck.

'Hoy! That's mine!' he shouted, as she yanked him forward by the string. The string snapped. The lady held the stone on her palm. 'Look!' she sneered. 'Land magic. A poor pebble that has never known the sea. It has been kissed and whispered over by some stupid little creature of the hills. So this is why you did not hear my warning, and swim away with the other one. But it has no power over me.' She popped the stone into her mouth like a bonbon, swallowed, and smiled at him again. 'No land magic can save you now, boy. For the tide is rising.'

And much to Egg's alarm, it was. The deepening

shadows swirled around him, and they were not shadows any more but sea. He flailed and kicked as it rose above his head, and realized that this was what Will had seen when he took flight. He tried to claw his way towards the distant surface as Will had done, but the lady seized him by his swirling ginger hair and held him down.

'Mother!' shouted Utterly. It was the first time she had called the lady that, and she wished it had been in happier circumstances – she did not want a mother who took such cold joy in drowning people. 'Mother, please don't!'

The lady ignored her, watching Egg's frightened face. She had seen this sea-change so many, many times yet it still amused her. How the boy's scared eyes did bulge! How prettily the bubbles poured from his mouth each time he gulped for air and took in only water. When he was dead she would hang him with the others in the deep.

'Mother,' said Utterly. 'I *want* to go home with him!'

The lady forgot about Egg. She looked at her daughter in astonishment, and just beneath the astonishment Utterly sensed a trembling anger rising. 'Utterly! You are of the sea, not the land.'

'Why? Why can I not belong to both?'

The lady's eyes had turned white, as if they had iced over. 'Utterly, I brought you home. Utterly, I gave you gifts. You are bound to me utterly, Utterly.'

'Blarrk,' gargled Egg, or words to that effect.

'I am sorry, Mother,' Utterly said. 'I cannot choose, I cannot! I love the sea *and* the land.' She remembered something she had read in the Gorm's book. She said, 'You wondered how mortals manage there, knowing they will die and the sea will eat the land up in the end? It is because they have friends, and families. They have pictures, and music, and stories. They have the earth and the things that grow in it, and they love it every bit as much as you love the sea. That is why I don't want to choose between the sea and the land. I love them both. But if you make me choose, then I have to choose Wildsea. It is where I have lived all my life. It is where I belong.'

Her mother did not understand her. How could she? The Gorm had been getting her own way since the first storm howled over the face of the first ocean. What did she know of friends or love or home? That was why all she had been able to offer Utterly were presents.

Utterly looked down at herself, at all the lovely things she wore, the gown of green silk, the jewelled rings. She looked at the bracelet of pink daisies tied around her wrist which had been the first of the lady's gifts, and was still Utterly's favourite. But gifts could bind you to the giver, and Utterly wished to be unbound.

Very deliberately she held up her hand so her mother could see, and took hold of the bracelet with the other, and broke it.

266

As the flowers fell around her feet, she realized they were not flowers at all, but pieces of pink coral.

'Utterly,' said the lady, with a sound like a little wave collapsing onto shingle.

She let go of Egg, who sank slowly to the floor and lay face down.

The lady's eyes faded to a warmer grey, then became softly blue again. Two salt tears spilled from them. She looked for a moment so lost and sad and infinitely lonely that Utterly felt tears in her own eyes too. Then the lady hung her head, and let her shoulders slump, and her knees give way. She crumpled like a puppet whose puppeteer has suddenly remembered he has somewhere else to be. She fell at Utterly's feet and lay there, just a poor drowned girl cast up on a floor of sea-damp sand, with her wet hair draped thickly across her face.

The hanging lamps fell too. They did not shatter, but landed with dull, heavy splats on the sand, or dropped like ugly wet hats upon the heads of statues. They were not lamps at all but just big, softly glowing jellyfish. The lovely chamber they had lit was only a sea cave on a lonely shore.

Utterly went to Egg. 'I'm drowned,' he said, cautiously moving his fingers in the sand. 'I think I must be.'

'No,' said Utterly. 'No, Egg. This is land, if we want it to be. It is land, and air. Please, Egg . . .'

He took in a great gulping breath, and then another,

then sat up and looked at Utterly. 'You have got a load of weed all over you,' he said.

Utterly looked down and saw that he was right. Her gorgeous green gown had turned into a mass of slimy weed, like Cinderella's ball dress turning back to rags when midnight chimed. The rings the lady had given her were just a cluster of hermit crabs clinging to her fingers. She tugged the weeds away and there was her own sea-spoiled calico dress underneath. She plucked off the crabs and tore the crown from her head to discover it was only a loop of limpet-studded rope.

Egg went to peer at the lady. 'Is she dead?' he asked.

'I don't think she can die,' said Utterly. 'Her mood changed, that is all. She will have taken on another form to match it.' But she was not sure what the Gorm's mood had changed *to*. What form would her Gormish grief take? And how quickly would it turn back into rage? Even now, in the deeps offshore, weed could be weaving into muscles, muscles into limbs . . .

'We'd best be gone then,' said Egg. 'She almost had me, though I proved too tough for her. Even I might not be able to cope with her if she turns into that weedy giant again. We need to find your uncle too. Aish will kill me if I let him drown.'

Outside the cave, in evening twilight, the tide was rushing in. The waves burst in white spray among the rocks. 'Go!' they roared at Utterly. '*Ungrateful child! Go, then! Go!*'

39

OPEN WATER

They stumbled together across steep slippery rocks to the cave mouth. Outside they found no trace of any mansions, only tall cliffs, sculpted by the sea into arches and pinnacles and towering lonely stacks. What had seemed stairways were just shining shelves of stone, and what had seemed gardens were only clumps of weed and coral. Egg took Utterly's hand and they helped one another over the tumble of the rocks and through the maze of tide-pools while the surf roared louder and louder. When Utterly looked back, she saw that where the mouth of the cave had been there was now nothing but sea, and sky, and the first stars coming out.

'The island is going away!' she said.

Egg turned to look. Gaps were yawning in the skyline. Stars and sea showed through them.

'It is as if we are only actors in a play,' said Utterly. 'And now it has turned out to have a different ending than the writer planned, she is dismantling all the scenery and rolling up the backdrops. I do wish she would let us get offstage first . . .' She wondered if she should call out to the Gorm and beg her for forgiveness, but the waves were smashing against the rocks with a fury that threw foam three storeys high, and Utterly did not think her mother was in a mood to listen.

They hurried on. All around them now the cliffs and rocks were blowing away like mist on a stiff breeze. The boulders underfoot lost their texture, as if they were forgetting they were supposed to be stone, or any solid thing at all.

'How far to your boat?' shouted Utterly, above the boom and hiss of the sea.

'Not far.'

Then Utterly set down her foot on what looked like shingle only for it to vanish under her and send her plunging into chilly water. She sank deep, and surfaced, spluttering, to find herself in the open sea.

Egg bobbed up nearby. They swam closer to each other and turned in circles, treading water inexpertly. Utterly hoped there might be some scrap of ground remaining on which they might crawl ashore. Egg prayed that the beach where the boat had been might have been spared, or at the very least the boat itself. But the whole island was gone.

'That old Gorm never planned for us to escape,' said Egg bitterly.

'I don't think she has *plans*, exactly,' said Utterly. 'She just has moods, like the sea does. Sometimes they are gentle moods, and sometimes they are angry.'

'But at the moment she is angry,' said Egg. He glanced from side to side and then behind him, for fear giant tentacles or weedy hands were rising from the waves to drag him down. 'She is angry at me for fetching you away, and angry at you for leaving.'

But Utterly was not so sure. She knew that in some vast, oceanic way the Gorm cared for her. She was not angry at Utterly, only at the choice Utterly had made.

They floated in silence for a while, rising and falling. There was a rhythm to it, as if they were resting on the chest of an immense and gently breathing animal. They quickly grew cold, and their teeth chattered. All around them the big waves shone like hills of sliding ice. And then one wave, even bigger than the rest, lifted them so high that Utterly could look across the tops of all the other waves and saw, not far off, the white diamond of a little sail.

'Egg!' she said, reaching out to shake him by the sodden shoulder of his shirt.

'Here! Over here!' they both cried, raising their cold hands to signal to the boat. They knew the boat had seen them, for they could see the sail fluttering as it changed course. They lost sight of it again, and then suddenly it was very close, slipping sideways down the slope of a wave at them. Egg grabbed the gunwale as it passed, and Utterly grabbed Egg.

Uncle Will leaned over the boat's side and helped them struggle aboard. 'Utterly! Egg!' he said, laughing with relief, or maybe weeping; it was hard to tell. 'Thank Heavens you are safe! I had thought—'

He stopped himself. He did not like to say it, but he had thought them both dead. When he came floundering to the surface he had found the island gone. He had dived again and again, hoping to find Egg, but there were no mansions under the waves any more. The Gorm had shut him out of her enchantments, and there was nothing but open water, dark and cold and frighteningly deep.

The only thing in sight that was not sea had been Thurza Froy's boat, empty and adrift, and not too far away for Will to swim to. He had been sailing circles in it ever since, looking down into the waves, hoping for glimpses of the Gorm's realm and finding none, while sometimes shouting, 'Utterly!' or, 'Egg!' He had been about to give up hope and turn for Wildsea when he saw the children waving.

He settled them in the boat and wrapped them in blankets which Mrs Skraeveling had thoughtfully stowed under the thwarts. 'I can scarce believe that you are safe,' he kept saying. 'It is like waking from a nightmare; all seemed lost, and now all is well again.'

'All *will* be well, as long as you know how to get us

back to Wildsea,' said Egg, through clattering teeth. 'We ain't home yet, and I wouldn't be s'prised if there was monsters out here.'

There *was* a monster. Utterly knew it. She could feel the Gorm watching from below as her uncle turned the boat around with much flapping of sailcloth. She sensed its tangled darkness looming like a sandbar just beneath the keel. A body of weed and shipwrecks big as a drowned mountain, and just as much her mother as the lady in white had been.

She looked west, to where the last light of the vanished sun still stained the sky, and saw that the whole sea was filled with islands. Some were low, some mountainous, some prickly with pine forests and crags. One isle seemed to stand above the waves on pillars, with sunlit cataracts pouring from its brim. On another, proud towers rose. Utterly stared, trying to take them all in, trying to fix them in her memory. She knew the Gorm was showing her all the Hidden Lands she might have visited, if only she had stayed. All the Hidden Lands she could still visit, if only she would return . . .

She is so lonely, Utterly thought, and tears blurred the islands' outlines. She felt like a murderer. She felt like an ungrateful girl who had broken her mother's heart.

She wiped her eyes, and when she looked again the light was gone, and the islands were gone with it, and the sea rolled empty to all horizons.

❖

Will sat at the tiller, while Egg and Utterly made their way forward and curled up out of the wind and spray in the little angle at the very front of the boat. It was really not a bad boat at all, and not too much water had seeped in, so Utterly lay there quite snug inside her blanket and thought about the sea. After a little while she sensed that the wind had changed direction. It was blowing from the west now, driving the boat easily across the waves. And after a while longer, when she lifted her head to peek over the side, she saw a light in the darkness ahead. It lay very low upon the eastern sky, and it looked too warm to be a star.

'Uncle Will!' she said. 'Look!'

'I know,' said Will, who had been watching it for twenty minutes. 'They have lit a lamp for us at Sundown Watch.'

The wind grew stronger, and the boat raced ahead of it. Will kept his eye on that light until the night faded and it was lost among the glories of the sunrise. But by that time he did not need a lamp to guide him home. He could see quite clearly the familiar hills of Wildsea rising from the waves.

40

HOME FROM THE SEA

Aish had been awake all night, tending the fire on the cliff's edge above Blanchmane's Cove. It was a good, golden fire of honest dry-land wood, and everyone had hoped it might guide the lost adventurers home. But one by one the Skraevelings and the Dearloves had grown sleepy and taken themselves off to their beds, till only Aish was left, carefully feeding logs into the flames.

When first light came and she saw the Hidden Lands were gone she almost lost hope entirely. When she spotted the sail, way out across the grey dawn sea, she thought her eyes were playing games with her.

Her excited shouts woke up the household. Mr Skraeveling and Reverend Dearlove lit lanterns, and carried them up onto the precarious stump of the Tower so that if Will kept the lanterns lined up with Aish's fire he would be able to steer the boat through the off-shore rocks and safe into the cove. Their wives carried blankets down the cliff. A crowd of onlookers from Marazea and the Dizzard and as far away as Merriport gathered with them there to watch the Watcher's return. When the boat ran up onto the shore they raised a loud cheer and when they saw that not only Egg but Utterly was safe aboard they raised an even louder one.

Lucy and Horatio joined the villagers wading bravely into the waves to haul the boat up the beach and help the homecoming mariners ashore. Mrs Skraeveling and Mrs Dearlove passed out the blankets, and sips of purely medicinal brandy. Aish lifted Egg off his feet and whirled him around for joy, then hugged Utterly so tight it felt as if she was trying to squeeze all the seawater out of her clothes. And when she came to Will she looked shy for a moment before she pulled him close and kissed him.

Will did not appear to mind, so it looked to Utterly as if Egg's prediction about Aish and her uncle being wed by summer might come true. She was not sure how that would work out, for she could not imagine Aish wanting to live in an ordinary house, or Uncle Will moving to the Dizzard, but she felt glad that Uncle Will would not be lonely any more. And she would be able to tell Lucy Dearlove 'I told you so', so on the whole it seemed a happy development.

There was talk of breakfast at Sundown Watch. 'Three cheers for Mr Dark!' cried Reverend Dearlove, raising his hat against the morning sky. 'And for Egg, and for Utterly Dark. They have defeated the sea! Hip, hip—'

'Huzzah!' the whole crowd cheered, moving up the beach. 'Huzzah! Huzzah!'

But Utterly lingered on the shore, and Will stayed with her. The waves at the mouth of the cove looked as black as old pewter under the pale dawn sky.

'The reverend is wrong,' said Will. 'The sea is not defeated. The Gorm is not defeated. But she did not drown us when she could have done. She let us sail safely home. No boat has ever sailed across the western deeps before, and touched the Hidden Lands, and come home safe to shore.'

'Yes,' said Utterly. And she wondered if the things she had said to the Gorm, which had felt so childish as she said them, had made more impression on the Gorm's strange heart than she had thought. 'I think she may be gentler now,' she said. 'I think there will be – not a friendship between the sea and the land, for that can never be – but perhaps a sort of truce, for a while.'

Will looked down at her. Was it possible that she was really the child of the Gorm, hatched out of a mermaid's purse? It seemed unlikely now; as unlikely as his fast-fading memories of the Hidden Lands. But he sensed her regret. 'I left Wildsea once myself,' he said gently.

'And I was very miserable indeed when I had to return. When I arrived at Sundown Watch and found you here it was a surprise to me, but I quickly saw that it is just as Mr Skraeveling once told me: you are exactly what this old place needs. You brighten it up like a sunbeam on a dreary afternoon. And where would I be without my Assistant Watcher? And who would rub the head of poor old Tortoise on the staircase if you were not here to do it, for my hands are grown too big.' He laughed, then grew solemn and said awkwardly, 'What I am trying to say, I suppose, is that you are very dear to me, Utterly Dark, and I am glad that you decided to come home.'

But I am dear to the Gorm too, thought Utterly. She *was* glad to be back at Sundown Watch. She knew part of her would miss it always if she went away. It was where she had grown up, and all the memories of her childhood lived in it. But she would not be a child for ever. She thought of those Hidden Lands the Gorm had shown her as the darkness fell: a sea full of islands, all waiting to be explored.

'*Utterly*,' said the gentle waves. '*Utterly*.' And she knew that one day, when she was ready, she would heed their call, and walk once more down the long slopes of Wildsea, and pass through the gardens of the deep to her mother's mansions in the west.

'Oh, come *on*, Will Dark!' called Egg, who was waiting

a little way up the beach with Aish. 'Come on, Utterly – or the breakfast will all be ate before we get there.'

So Will lifted Utterly up and settled her on his shoulders, and they climbed the cliff path with Aish holding Will's hand and Egg running on ahead, and then they all went together across the lawns towards the lights and laughter of the house.

Behind them in the cove the beach lay empty, and the sea watched, and waited.

ACKNOWLEDGEMENTS

This book took a long time to come together, and might never have made it without the help and wise advice of my agent, Philippa Milnes-Smith, my editor, Liz Cross, and my excellent friend Sarah McIntyre, who always reads my stories before anyone else, and gets so enthusiastic about them that I have to keep going. (All my books are Reeve & McIntyre books now.) Thanks also to Paddy Donnelly for the beautiful cover and illustrations, to Sue Cook and Julia Bruce for proof-reading and copy-editing, and to everyone at DFB for giving Utterly a home. And, of course and as always, to Sarah Reeve, who kept our little island here on Dartmoor safe and snug and good to write in while the wild seas of 2020 raged all around.

Philip Reeve

ABOUT THE AUTHOR

Philip Reeve is the author of many acclaimed and bestselling books, including *Railhead*, *Here Lies Arthur* and *Mortal Engines*, which was made into a major movie. He has also collaborated with Sarah McIntyre on several hugely popular, highly-illustrated stories including *Pugs of the Frozen North* and the *Roly-Poly Flying Pony* series. His books have won the Carnegie Medal, the Smarties Prize and many other awards. He lives with his wife and son on Dartmoor.